TINY

tales

An Anthology of Delicious Paranormal & Fantasy Shorts

Collected from an Elite Assortment of Today's Best Up-And-Coming Writers, Edited by Batya Dulos

TINY TALES
An Anthology of Delicious Paranormal & Fantasy Shorts
Edited by Batya Dulos

ISBN: 978-1-7340474-9-3
Kindle ASIN: B08JQ8BQMK

Cover Image: © Depositphotos.com/liqwer20
Cover Design: Hyliaan Graphics

PUBLISHED IN THE UNITED STATES OF AMERICA

A Note from the Editor:

"A year ago, when Run Rabbit Books hired me on, I dove in with great pleasure, on location, poring through submissions with glee. Very soon after, the worldwide pandemic forced all of us to figure out how to work at home. One night, I had an idea for this anthology and we sent out a call. I asked for altered fairy tales and anything to do with vampires, witches, and paranormal ilk, word count from 500 to 3000 words. This book contains a little of all, so enjoy! I surely enjoyed compiling these tales for you!"

~ Batya Dulos, Editor, Run Rabbit Books
www.RunRabbitBooksLRPImprint.com

Table of Contents

Tiny tales

An Anthology of Delicious Paranormal & Fantasy Shorts

1

Plan A

Elizabeth E. Little

Plan A was always *don't confront the monster.*

Plan B, on the other hand, was usually *well, Plan A failed, so I guess it's time to die.*

With plan-making abilities of that caliber, Arthur was committed to making sure Plan A never, *ever* failed. It was what had made him so successful in the field, the secret of his trade, so to speak. While knights gamely traversed the countryside killing wyverns or griffons or what have you, brandishing broadswords and shields and shining with the light of their magnificence, Arthur was the sort who'd rather sneak around the back and get out while the getting was good. If that made him a little bit of a coward, well, at least cowards got to live.

So as he crouched behind the low stone wall surrounding a truly *magnificent* killing field, Arthur went over everything he'd need to do to make sure Plan A was the only plan he'd be following. You see, people only came to Arthur when *their* Plan A (and usually their Plans B through G, too) failed. Arthur wasn't a knight. The sum total of his knowledge of swords was "sharp end goes into enemy," and the less said about his archery the better. But what Arthur was *good* at, other than harboring a truly impressive survival instinct, was getting in and out of places guarded by things that routinely treated human beings like crunchy snacks.

Now, Arthur wasn't one to *judge*, exactly… well no, that's a lie. Arthur judged his clients *a lot.* Especially this kind; the kind where an uppity princeling, or lord, or well-to-do merchant baron had found a nice piece on the side, only that piece turned out to be a long-lost princess of an ancient forest king or some shit, and that ancient forest king didn't much like the idea of his precious princess lowering herself to sleep with a random moron whose only defining trait was having three gold pieces to rub together.

So instead of doing something *reasonable*, like a *normal person*, the king would jump right towards imprisoning his precious snowflake in a tower in the middle of Merlin-be-damned *nowhere.* Because assassinating the offending man would be *way* too sane of an option, and heaven forbid there be any handy *dungeons* lying around in their *massive kingdom* where they could store their rebellious offspring without the need for her to be guarded by *monstrosities.*

Arthur took a calming breath. Now was not the time to get into this again, not when he was within spitting distance of the most recent example of human stupidity. He didn't really care who the client was, only that they were willing to pay half his fee up front and seemed hopelessly besotted with the idea of whatever unfortunate woman was locked in that tower, smack dab in the middle of this huge clearing riddled with craters and bones, and surrounded by a truly ominous ring of spiked mountains. As if things weren't exciting *enough*, it was now overcast and threatening to rain.

Arthur was not a knight. It was *not his job* to go down there, bellow a challenge into the void, and see what unholy nightmare crawled out of the stones to answer it. *His* job was to get to the tower, retrieve the pretty princess, and get the hell out while he still had all his limbs. He was not, of course, the first idiot to be trying this. There were too many bones scattered around the field below him for *that* little fantasy to hold weight. The client hadn't had really even known what sort of hellspawn this particular king had cursed / bribed / persuaded into guarding the tower, but it was probably a dragon.

Because idiot kings with idiot daughters were clichéd like that.

Arthur squinted. There weren't a lot of places for a dragon to hide down there, he conceded dubiously. The killing field was very open, and the tower itself was mostly just a stack of rocks with a roof on it. It could be in the mountains, he guessed, watching over the clearing like a vulture. Or if he was *supremely* unfortunate it might be an Earthwyrm and be right under his feet even now.

And that's only if this whatever-it-was was a dragon *at all*, and Arthur wasn't discounting the fact that it might not be. Despite the fact that dragons were usually the first, last, and only thing most people thought of when they thought of *guardian monster*, that didn't mean this couldn't have been the one time an idiot king had a flash of *actual intelligence* and picked something else.

Arthur knew it wasn't a hellhound; it would have smelled him by now despite the myriad of scent-repelling and concealment enchantments woven through his clothing. It probably wasn't a griffon or a wyvern, because those were both very vain creatures and they would have been doing somersaults in the air or something to show off their feathers or scales or claws or whatnot. By that merit he could rule out dryads and nymphs too, and not only because this place was absolutely devoid of trees or water.

He very much doubted it was a fae. Faeries couldn't be coerced into doing things, and they had a disdain for mortals that Arthur thanked the gods for every time he went out on a job. If people had *fae* guarding things, Arthur would just hang up his cloak and stay inside for the rest of his natural life. Going up against a fae was a great way to find yourself trapped a million years in the past or spliced across sixteen dimensions inhospitable to human life.

And neither of those assertions are facetious.

Arthur took another steadying breath, readied the satchel containing the items he'd need to use to scale the tower (because doors were *obviously* not something you'd want to install on a tower your *flesh and blood* would be living in, why bother hiding the fact they're a prisoner?), and hopped quietly over the wall.

So far so good. Nothing had burst up from below to eat him, and nothing was stirring in the mountains. He kept his eyes peeled regardless. He carefully avoided stepping on any bones (more because of the noise they'd make rather than out of respect he felt for idiots who charged headfirst into killing fields) and tiptoed through the tulips right past what he'd dubbed The Threshold.

The Threshold was what he had judged to be the point of no return, where he couldn't feasibly outrun something if it decided to make its presence known. Oh sure he could still run like hell, but he was far enough from the wall now that if it was locked to this clearing in the way he sort of figured it would be (had to keep their pet monsters guarding the tower *somehow*) that his odds of making it were slim.

He had a few tricks left up his sleeve just in case, he wasn't an *amateur*, but it still put him on even higher alert than he'd been literally two seconds before. If a monster was going to leap out of the woodwork and cinch the dramatic timing, it was going to be now.

Arthur strained his ears, muscles tensed as he picked up the pace, uneasy with how smoothly things were going. Usually he'd be hip-deep in magical traps or imps or the like by now. Surely there were actual defenses around the tower? Not even the stupidest of dense kings would rely on *only* a monster to keep their daughter's virtue safe. Right?

He made it all the way to the base of the tower without a single thing flinging itself at him teeth-first. Arthur relaxed his guard a little. Maybe the monster was asleep? Or dead, it might be dead. Maybe one of these unfortunate idiots back in the killing field had managed to wound it before dying? He guessed he was due a bit of good luck by now, after the string of truly unfortunate mishaps dotting his previous few runs.

He dug around in his satchel until he found the pick he used to scale sheer walls—it was enchanted to never dull or lose its grip on the rock until pulled at a certain angle that couldn't be managed while falling. Truly one of his best purchases. Arthur steadied himself and swung the pick at the stonework, ready to get in and get out while things were still going smoothly.

The sound the metal made as it hit the rock was *deafening*. Arthur cringed, immediately letting go of the pickaxe and leaping away on sheer instinct, knowing nothing that loud could possibly be good or natural, and sprinted for the distant wall. The sound was still echoing, growing louder and louder as it bounced off the mountains around them, and Arthur cursed himself and his client and whoever spelled the tower to do that to the pits of *hell* because that was *clever,* damn it, and Arthur hated himself a little for being grudgingly respectful.

Why riddle the clearing with traps if you could just rig the damn tower to ring like a gong if it's touched?

Then the earth started shaking. Arthur didn't look back, not wanting to see what this unholy racket was waking up, but that didn't exactly help when the bloody *mountains started moving.* Arthur froze, stumbling as his momentum abruptly canceled itself, as he stared with in wide-eyed horror at the fucking *mountain range* that was *not a mountain range at all fuck his life.*

The spiked peaks heaved and ground against each other like the blades of a saw, shifting in a wave of motion as they lifted clear off the ground on the spine of a creature so large Arthur couldn't even wrap his mind around it. Curled around the entirety of the clearing, the monster rocked to feet tipped with claws that even from this distance, over a mile away, he could see every gleaming obsidian inch. The creature was so impossibly massive that Arthur couldn't quite make himself believe it was real, as if his mind was playing tricks on him.

It unfolded, swinging around to face him and that's when he saw the iconic head, the spiraling horns that had once been the twisted pair of peaks bracketing the entrance of the valley, the jagged crags of teeth and bulwark-scales the size of houses. That's when he saw the huge backwards-jointed legs, the miles-long whip-like tail tipped in sharp peaks, the way its jaws parted and its throat glowed orange as molten drool fell from between serrated teeth, the way the cracks between its scales bled lava and all twelve of its eyes burned with hellfire. That was when Arthur calmly reached into his satchel, mind buzzing with white noise and ears ringing with the gong of the tower and the cracking roll of the dragon's joints grinding into each other like a landslide, and pulled out Plan C.

Sir Horton,

Fuck you. Fuck your princess, and fuck your gold, and fuck your stupid mustache while you're at it. Here's your down payment back. Keep it with my fucking blessings. That's a fucking Lava Elemental *guarding your fucking pretty princess and* good fucking luck *finding some idiot stupid enough to go fight it.*

Fucking Sincerely,
Arthur

Grunt Work: 401

DH Lee & Emil Stern

The redhead has been staring at me for ten minutes. I'm nothing to look at, medium height, medium complexion, medium build, just a blah dude. A quick peripheral glance and she's still looking in my direction, her green-eyed gaze boring a hole in my right cheek. This is my first night to sit in the target's class, so maybe my "newness" attracted her. I sat down thirty-two minutes ago, and I swear she's been eyeing me most of that time.

What does she look like, you wonder?

Do you mean to me or to you?

I see a blob of hair and tissue, the frizz on top is orange which is why I call her the Redhead. You'd think she was petite, feminine, and pretty, if not a little too fragile for this Forensics Criminology 101 course.

HOLY FUCK! She can't keep her eyes off of me. SHIT!

Her attention *draws* attention and I'm trying to go unnoticed. Be invisible. Of course, I can't *be invisible*—I'm in a flesh-suit, it's three-dimensional. There are people in my organization who wear hybrid-flesh-suits and they can bend light in such a way to seem to disappear. But that's not me.

Okay, she looked away. The professor is speaking on his topic and I stare at the back of my target's head. My mission is simple – destroy my target without touching him. Yeah, that's a stupid way to do it, but I didn't write the rulebook. I'm a grunt. I follow. And I'm damn good at my job. Also, I have never failed.

NO FRICKKIN' WAY. The Redhead has turned her head again. She is sending me a smile. I don't look at her, I won't, but my peripheral vision works just fine. Fuck her, I'm working. I concentrate on my target. Tonight is my fourth attempt to destroy him. He hasn't made it easy. Luckily, he is not popular; multiple familial and social connections make it more difficult get close enough to perform my task. This guy has almost nobody.

The target's an average student making average decisions on what to eat and what to wear, nothing stands out about him, not his face, not his personality. This target lives alone with his widowed father, a man who works three jobs and still can't afford a car. Which is why my first attempt took place on my target's long walk home in the dark after class.

I mentioned to you this was my fourth attempt. That means three times I have missed. I normally get this right the first time, and at the most, the second, so it is odd that I would miss. Attempt #1 was when he was walking home from this class. My detailed reconnaissance revealed he had no car. His poverty was extensive; he was at school on a scholarship and his father was so behind on his bills that they could barely afford groceries. I've seen this boy sneak leftovers off trays left behind by eaters. So, on my first attempt, I expected this to go fine.

He had been walking home in the dark, along the sidewalk, on a quiet strip where the mom & pop businesses had closed for the night. I trailed twenty-five feet behind him, the maximum distance for me to project my will onto his. I strolled with nonchalance in case he should look back. But he didn't. I began with what had worked with previous similar targets in the past.

"I am a terrible son. I can't do anything right," I sent over the airwaves. He would pick them up, and with my expertise, he'd think they were his own thoughts. *"I'm a drain on my father. If I wasn't around, Dad wouldn't have to worry over me day and night, worry about providing for his only child. If I wasn't around, Dad would be so much better off…"*

My associates had scheduled a truck, so I had a precise timetable. I continued to send my suggestions, watching and "feeling" for the oncoming semi.

"I'd be better off dead. Dad could get by so much better if I wasn't there needing shit all the time…"

The target walked slower and slower, his shoulders drooped, his head lowered, and the tractor-trailer zoomed into the box.

"I should just step in front of that truck. Fast. Painless…"

My sentiments continued to deliver, and the target turned his face to the headlights. In the past, my targets usually did what I suggested, but this one paused to think. I rolled my eyes; I've seen this before. This guy had begun to doubt the little voice in his head. He did not step off the curb into the road. The truck barreled harmlessly past. The target stopped walking and turned to look behind him. I gave him a wave and turned perpendicular, this road leading between two closed businesses. The spell had broken. The target hurried on home and I did as well, already planning attempt #2.

The second and third attempts were similar, but instead of doing it on the sidewalk, I allowed him to reach his house. I peeked at him through the window and spoke to his mind from there. Much like your Hollywood movies, I could not go in without being invited. The only loophole is if the homeowner(s) had been inviting my ilk inside already, *they* could let me in, but this asshole kept a clean place and I had to do my job outdoors.

I don't care. So what. No hill for a climber.

The 2nd attempt, I heard him arguing with his father and he stormed off to the tiny home's only bathroom. From the opaque glass set in the shower wall, I sent, *"I'm such a loser! I need to kill myself. Look… Dad's prescriptions. That would do it…"*

The target opened the medicine cabinet and read the labels of the first few bottles. Before he opened any of them, he looked into the mirror and doubted the voice was his own.

I scooted home. Denied.

Next night, the 3rd attempt, I came back to the house and caught him and his father cleaning their armory. As bumpkins like to do, they had amassed quite an arsenal including Army ordinance. I sort of wished this was an assignment where we'd blow some people up, but I needed to focus. My boss wanted this target dead and I shouldn't waste time fantasizing bigger jobs or coveting the missions of those who have them.

"This one has two safeties; it won't fire unless you're actually holding it properly," the dad was saying to the target, holding up a semi-automatic pistol. "I used to have a Glock, but sold it when your mom died…"

From my hiding place outside the living room window, I grinned. The target's mother died in childbirth.

"It should have been me. Dad loved her so much… It should have been me," I sent and watched the young man avert his eyes and leave the room, SigSauer in hand. Once he

was alone, I sent a few more.

"I'll just do it this way. I'll shoot myself. Daddy will be so much better off. If I did it just right, maybe it would look like an accident and Dad could collect a bunch of insurance money…"

I watched and waited.

"Naw, fuck-it…"

The target put the barrel to his temple. I smiled my plain-jane (jim?) host's mouth.

Shit.

He set down the gun and went to the toilet to piss. Facing the wall, I heard him say in a low hiss, *"Get thee behind me satan! I belong to the Lord!"*

Shit-a-brick-fuck-a-lick-tit.

Now he revealed his secret. I'd need to go to Defcon 1 for my next attempt. I backed away from the house and walked past the living room. That asshole father was reading from a leather-bound book, probably a Bible or Tanakh[1]—some religious book. Probably not a Koran because these two are so redneck.

So… I missed a 3rd time.

I wasn't depressed. This time, tonight, before the boy even made it to the campus lawn, I would have him do it. There's no limit on the number of times I can *try* but there is a limit of time before he starts "calling out the devil" every time I get close. If he recognizes my voice, which he may now, my mission is over, and they will have to send somebody else. Somebody with a different style, with a different voice, a different feel. I really couldn't fail this time. That's why I'm sitting here, behind him in the classroom.

The redhead is still looking at me, now she's making goo-goo eyes. Does this host look like someone she knows? Fuck, that would be weird, huh? I'm still not looking directly at her. I don't want to encourage that

[1] Jewish Scriptures, includes the five books of Torah plus The Writings.

crazy witch.

Did she just wave her fingers? She's in love with this host. I don't know anything about this body they gave me but it would be really funny if she knew him.

Continuing on...

Suddenly, I got a communication from my superiors. I had to smile. I'm sure they don't like me and they probably don't respect me, but they respect my numbers, and for whatever reason, they decided not to give me this piece of information until now.

Newsflash: there had been 400 of my ilk assigned before now. I was number 401 sent to destroy this target. Consider that, this boy was nineteen years old. Over nineteen years, FOUR HUNDRED before me have failed to destroy this target.

What's so fucking special about this one? When we're sent to destroy you, it's easy. Why did the boss keep trying? Just give up. Let him alone. I could catch a hundred targets in the time it's taken me to fail three times on this one.

But, I won't fail this time. I know my enemy. I know he has this hedge around him and I will punch through it here, at school, and far away from his holy books and holy dad. This communication regarding Grunt Work 401 means I will have to pull out all the stops. Everything I have learned over three millennia with every target in every generation will need to be examined so I can destroy him. To add to the drama, this is my last shot. After tonight, he will call me out every time I say one word.

The redhead is walking over here. She has no shame, coming over as if she'd been invited.

She stopped a few feet away and asked if she could borrow a pencil. I don't look up; I can't look at her, as a matter of fact. One of the things that we do not like to do is make eye contact except with our target.

I reach blindly around in the desk compartment and pull out the first thing I grab. It's an ink pen. I handed it to her still averting my gaze.

She sighed and said, "Will you look again? I really need a pencil. I'm writing a letter to my mom and I made a mistake. My pencil's eraser is all used up. You see, my mom is suffering with gout and she can't get any relief."

She stopped making words and I had not reached in the desk a second time. Will she go away? Hell no.

"Will you look again?" she repeated then.

Time, which has no meaning in my dimension, means everything in yours. The clock on the wall and in this plane was ticking, the professor was closing out the lecture, and soon, everyone would be leaving. I needed to get the boy while he was in the bathroom. That's where he would go next, to the men's room to piss before the long walk home. I would meet him with a posse of 2000 compatriots, all arriving now as a favor to me. There is zero doubt that all of us together will convince this target to destroy himself.

"She didn't know it was gout for the longest time and it seemed everything she ate brought her immense pain…"

This young woman will not stop talking to me until I get her a blasted pencil. I did not bring a pencil on this assignment and had no confidence this borrowed desk contained one, but I dug around with an exaggerated snarl on my host's lips. My fingers closed on another writing utensil – a Sharpie.

SAVED! The professor noticed the redhead and asked her to kindly find her seat.

"I will as soon as I get a pencil," she said, her eyes on me and not the prof.

CRUD-MONKEYS! I needed her to sit down. I

made a decision. I would reply. A single word. It was risky, but I said low, "Sorry."

Why is this a big deal? Because this body is dead. I am constantly—with amazing ability and finesse—reanimating it to make it move and appear alive. It takes tons of concentration, but I am able to tamp down the odor of decay as I animate the limbs. To conserve energy, I don't operate the vocal cords. But when uttered that lonely word, it sounded raspy, strange, and probably *inhuman.*

I could have exploded with frustration in the next moment because the redhead put her hand to my upper back and asked, "Are you okay? Are you crying?"

F-U-C-K!!!!!

The professor was busily announcing tomorrow's assignment, students were gathering their belongings and getting to their feet, some were milling toward the exit, and this redhead had me pinned to the desk.

THERE ARE SO MANY FUCKING RULES! And one of these is NO contact with your kind. She couldn't have known, but this rule is the main reason others in my organization will refuse an assignment that requires a flesh-suit. Most of my ilk would rather take on the mission bodiless, where hundreds, or thousands (or millions, if required) band together to affect a change in the three-dimensional world. Granted, in a flesh-suit, we can perform everything faster and easier, but the rules and the risks…

Here was the biggie.

The redhead innocently touched the host's back, and until she lifted her hand, I was grounded in place. I literally *could not move.* I sent my memory back to seek out the best solution. I'd been at this job for 3000 years and possessed a bank full of information to resolve any calamity. I chose the one that worked most often.

I would utter a phrase and she would go away. I carefully formed the words and pushed them from my rotting lungs. Because of my limitations of voice, I could produce syllables, but not separate the words. My reply rolled into one weird word, but she should be able to comprehend it. I mean, shit.

"M'Fine."

The hand remained.

In my peripheral vision, the class was walking out, and my target was speaking to the professor. The redhead asked me if I needed some water.

"I noticed you were really quiet. Would you like for me to sit with you for a while? Are you depressed? Because I know a lot about that. I could help you. Can we be friends?"

Again, I searched for a strategic response. I needed this girl to lift her hand so I could scoot out of that room. The contact had remained now for over thirty seconds and I was beginning to drain out. My essence had focused on the fold, which is an opening in the dimension wall. I could slip right on through if I didn't get that mother-fucking hand off my back.

I didn't want to go. I couldn't afford to fail.

I focused every iota of my remaining energy on the host's rubbery vocal cords to say two distinct words designed to cause her to remove her hand. I muttered in a dry gasp, "Water, please."

Nope.

The hand remained.

The redhead reached into her shoulder bag and pulled out a bottled water, the contact not moving an inch. The target left the room and the professor switched off the lights, calling out, "Let's go, cleaning crew's coming in!"

This left the two of us in the dark, me at the desk, a

bottle of water lax in my right hand, the redhead standing beside me, her hand to my back and leaning down, concerned for the guy she saw before her.

She stroked the host's shirt, up and back, without breaking contact. She cooed, "Do you need any help? You seem really sick."

Tick-tock-tick. Four minutes elapsed and she was still there. I was nearly gone and every minion in the quadrant was laughing their asses off at my debacle.

A male poked his head in to ask if we were okay and the redhead said, "We're fine, thank you. He was feeling a little bit dry, so I brought in some water. Will be out in just a minute."

Whoever it was said okay and left us alone. The room fell very quiet and the redhead continued to rub my back, every now and then asking if I was feeling better.

I'm moments from going back. The slip in the fold called me, pulling me through, and most of me had listened and whispered away.

I'M NOT DONE…

I had one more trick. There was a word that females found more offensive than any other. She should break contact in disgust. I could recall my elements if she lifted her hand now. I wasn't fully gone...

I sent my waning energy to my host's throat and said as plainly as possible, "cunt."

"Punt?" she said in the same sweet voice. "Oh! You play football? I get it. You're feeling down and this was sort of a punt, wasn't it? Well, don't you worry. I'm with you. I won't leave you alone until you're feeling better. That makes me your, what? Wide receiver? Huh, I don't know much about sports…"

That was it. The end of my energy.

The slip grew longer and brighter as my atoms

seeped into the void. My consciousness would return on the other side, but I would have no body. Instead, I would return to the collective where we spend most of our existence.

But wait.

Her words…

The read head switched languages. That's… that's ancient… that's *malakim,*[2] my first language.

"Tell your boss," she said in a conspiratorial whisper leaning close to my host's head, "you lose."

FUCK ME. She's a Guardian, one of those that work for the other team. *Shit…* I didn't see it. I can't see them like they can see us. Another rule I didn't make, and I can't control.

There you have it.

Your hero has failed.

The target goes on until they find a new patsy to enter a flesh-suit for Grunt Work 402. I will turn in my report, inform my superiors that the next grunt should try to get the target when he's away from home. His dad keeps the house hedged up and so far, the target hasn't established any sort of protection around himself when away from home. They'll get him.

Probably.

I won't know about it. I go back to the collective, get back in line for a turn in the flesh. I love that job. I'm good at it. I'll never give up and I hate this black mark on my record. But shit. No big whoop. I'll make it up. After all, I have all the time in the world.

---

[2] Derived from "malachim." Plural for "angel" or "messenger," in Hebrew.

3

A Vampire's First Love

Emil Stern

I came into the world in 1710, born a Rakum (you would call us "vampires"), and at age nine, my masters discovered I was born "ish-mikhan," a Rakum word for "fix-it man." This meant I possessed innate skill in the ways of sexually pleasing my Elders. I was favored and spoiled in every assignment but allow me to share on my favorite topic: Elder Canaan.

The following event occurred in 1932, when I met the master I would hold in my heart for the rest of my days. Jersey wrote about it from Canaan's perspective in his memoir, *Blood, Sex & Violence, A Vampire's Rebuttal* and now you shall see what I was thinking when this amazing man entered my timeline. Please, allow me to tell you how it really went.

Ken and Yan had been assigned to the Elder as soldiers, and although I was a captain by then and outranked them, Elder Bel, my master, assured me my role was to be strictly sexual. He held an affinity for Elder Canaan and enjoyed his company when we gathered. One thing he shared was that Canaan had little interest in fucking, no matter who offered; he had reached an age where he'd rather fight than anything else. Bel told me, "He had a valet before he graduated to Elder and you remind me of him. Not in looks—Judas Priest, no one looks like Darcy Vandiver—but in personality, joviality, likable nature. If Canaan sees you and doesn't instantly bend you over, he'll do it shortly after. He will not be able to resist you. And Darcy, listen. I want you to lay it on heavy. This Elder needs to breathe this aura you exude. Do you understand?"

I assured Master Bel that I would do as he instructed and me and my two escorts headed away. The trip was long and when we reached the city, we ducked into a Rakum waystation to freshen up. Ken and Yan spent most of the journey pretending I wasn't there, which was fine with me. They hadn't been instructed to stay off the ish-mikhan; it was their choice. Because of their indifference, by the time we reached the safehouse, I'd gone seventy-two hours without sex. This was on my mind as Ken walked ahead of me through the double doors of the building.

"There's a brother here named Geoffrey. He'll fuck you," Yan said as he passed my position and disappeared with Ken into the hall and out of sight. I stood in the center of the main room, sniffing out the shower since those two assholes didn't bother to help me find it.

Geoffrey…

I hadn't heard of him. I inhaled again, sorting the aromas, my own being the most offensive. I needed to wash and fast. Elder Canaan expected us soon and an ish-mikhan should never be late. I chose a hallway that smelled most of bleach and headed down. A shower started up and I realized I had chosen well. I reached a closed door and pushed it open.

"Kazak,"[3] the brother in the shower called without knowing who had entered. The steam prevented me

[3] Rakum greeting, means literally, "be strong."

from seeing his face and I called a greeting as I peeled off my shirt. There was one shower head, so the guy would need to get out or share. Before you ponder too long, Rakum are raised communally; we ate, slept, and bathed together since we were weaned. For this reason, the brother in the shower did not turn as he heard me clomp off my shoes and slide open the glass door to join him in the tight space. There was enough room for two, but not three.

"I'm done, just had to rinse off," the guy said and moved aside for me to take the lead.

Because of my nature, I looked upon him as I scooched around. He wasn't quite six feet, with bronzed skin, black hair and a razor-thin mustache. He raised his eyes to mine—deep brown, almost black, in a handsome, chiseled face. I felt my grin tuck into my cheek and he reflected the move.

"A fix-it man," he said as a statement and stopped the effort of leaving the stall. He squared up and took his time considering me from chin to toes. "Can you read grunts or just Elders?"

My smile widened because what I read was extremely interesting. Not only had Geoffrey been with ish-mikhan, he'd been with Jersey. And *a lot.* If you haven't read Jersey's memoir, I'll clue you in—Jersey mentored me. My first Elder held me close until I was seventy and then he sent me off to Elder Emil. The way the world works, on the way to Emil, my trip was hijacked by another Elder—Master Kilmeade—who we all considered the greatest of all Elders. He took me to his estate where he put me with his ish-mikhan, Jersey. He wanted to see if we would be compatible. Judas Priest, were we compatible! *Fuck!* (I promise; you'll hear more on this later in the book)

When I looked into Geoffrey's mind and saw

Jersey, I went on full-staff. He noticed and grinned. With nonchalance, his right hand took hold of my erection. In the first two seconds, I recognized the move he applied. Without going into too much detail, suffice it to say there are ways to move one's fingers on a circumcised man, and Geoffrey had been instructed well. Rakum grunts retain their foreskin (only the Fathers, Elders and ish-mikhan are circumcised) so his amazing skill meant Jersey spent a good amount of time explaining how to please.

"You like that," Geoffrey said and stepped closer as if to ask for a kiss.

I allowed him to get right under my nose, the hot water jets slamming my back and then I shook my head. "I'm on a mission, brother," I told him in my sexiest voice. "But you can wash me. I'd like that."

I wasn't asking. It's complicated to mortals, but several things were going on at the same time. I'll break it down for you because I want to, and this is my book. Geoffrey had been spoiled by Jersey, and his technique, no matter how flawless, could not make up for his arrogance. Add to that, I outranked him. Geoffrey wasn't a soldier, and I was, so I was his master. *Also,* I was a century older, which also made me his master. On top of all that, I hadn't been instructed to pleasure the guy. I considered all this as he pondered his next move. I knew what I wanted. My muse, the ish-mikhan spirit inside, wanted this condescending ass-wipe to bathe me. He was going to *please me.* I waited, another moment passed, and he finally slow-blinked.

"Your will is my will," Geoffrey said holding my eye, his delightful massage leaving my member to reach for the soap. For the next eleven minutes, Geoffrey of the South Street Waystation washed the fix-it man, and since I was being prepared to visit an Elder, he took extra care with every element of his duty. When I was as clean as a man can be, he shut off the water and stood facing me, both of us dripping and I expected him to commence the toweling off. Instead, he asked, "Will you be sleeping here when you finish with the Elder? I'll watch for you."

"This is outside of my control, but feel free to wait," I said. I needed to turn the blade. I mean, he'd been such a cocky prick—grunts are supposed to *venerate* me, not work an angle to get me to bed. I brought my hands up to frame his face, and this is the first time I'd touched him. His eyes grew soft and he parted his lips.

"Yes?" he whispered.

"If I come back here, I'll sleep in your quarters and show you everything Jersey held back. How does that sound?" I dug around in his gaze until we locked eyes hard and he could not look away. He also couldn't speak, his body online in a heartbeat. I waited another long second and kissed his forehead before leaving the stall. I did not allow him to towel me and I left the room, naked and dripping water. Was it showy? Yes. Was it cruel? I'd say so. I walked to the main room and called for my escorts to bring a towel along with my clothes. They did so after a minute and down the hallway, Geoffrey worked out his love pain all by himself.

"Darcy, you're such a shit," Yan said as I dried off and then reached for the dress slacks he held out. The three of us would present ourselves to the unfamiliar Elder in our best suits and my two escorts were clean, dressed, and had fed on some Cow[4] I never saw, distracted as I had been with Geoff.

"I am what I am," I whispered with a sideways smile. Yan had never met Elder Kilmeade, but this was

---

[4] A mortal viscerally drawn to give over his or her blood and body to my people.

his signature phrase and those of us who knew him loved to repeat it. I slipped on the Egyptian cotton shirt, and once buttoned, I flipped the tailored coat over one arm. "I'm ready."

"About damn time," Ken complained from the door. He clicked his tongue and we followed him out.

I took my place in the backseat, enjoying the sensation of being chauffeured. The two soldiers didn't mind; they enjoyed their job and they enjoyed each other. This is why they found it so easy to resist their beautiful companion. I watched them send each other laughing glances and secret nods like shit-eating mortals. Their behavior would have an Elder in fits of rage, but I wouldn't tell. I rarely saw such affection between brothers and I let them have it, my mind on Elder Canaan.

I had asked around once I knew we were headed to his abode. His reputation was one of bullish, cantankerous provocation. This didn't faze me—how many Elders were gentle kittens? *Zero.* Every grunt I questioned said Canaan smashed them, and not only that, but once smashed, he ground them into the dirt with his heel. I also loved violence—especially before sex. This caused me to smile, and Ken, who piloted us through the dark streets, caught my movement in the rearview mirror.

"Check his lap. Shit, he's jumping out of his skin."

"Leave him alone—they love Elders," Yan said with a tiny glance my way. "It's insane, but…"

I smiled to the side and looked out the car window. Our population regarded the One Hundred to be a posse of gigantic assholes. But the ish-mikhan? Elders were my very *life.* Plus, Ken was right. I *was* counting the minutes.

Elder Canaan…

He was said to be big and muscled, but not enormous like Elder Bel. Also, he had been proselytized by Elder Jack Dawn, so I could expect him to be especially pugilistic. I huffed to myself in the dark interior; I had only asked about him to tickle my anticipation. When my eyes landed in his, my muse (the ish-mikhan spirit inside of me) would tell me what to do. It was 100% reliable.

We finally arrived and headed up, the Elder residing in a tri-level apartment building. Mortals thought the rooms were inhabited by their kind, but in truth, only Rakum lived there. We don't trust humans to know where we sleep, so the place was heavily barricaded during the day and all of my brethren slept below ground in a light-tight barricaded cellar.

This night, as we entered the ground floor front door, a brother met us and showed us to the receiving chamber. A door was yanked open to reveal a twelve-by-twelve foyer. Once Ken, Yan, and I entered, a soldier joined us from the inner rooms. He spoke to my escorts, but I don't know what he said. My mind had turned to Elder Canaan. I couldn't see him, and I didn't know his scent, but my muse had locked onto his thread causing my skin to twitch. My breath grew shallow and my pulse increased. The chatty-Cathy called Tork served as the Elder's top lieutenant and he soon stepped up to me, asking inane questions I ignored. He yammered on, teasing me, trying to draw my ire, and just before I squashed him for his impudence, he turned away, instructing us to wait to be called.

"The Fathers must think you're lonely..." That was Tork speaking to his master in the other room. I remained behind my escorts, but my muse sang louder in my ears.

"Send them in, idiot," the Elder replied, and Ken and Yan started forward.

My muse began stroking the master's psyche even before I met his eye, so when he saw me, we both felt as if we'd already met. How do I write how magnificent this man was to my eyes this night? I consider myself a decent wordsmith, but are there phrases in the English language to describe this moment? In Rakum Hungarian, I'd say, *l'plzc karn'v lolz,* a sentiment that means basically, *Darcy died and was brought back to life simply by connecting eyes with this master.*

Melodramatic, eh? As you'll learn, I'm a romantic. Jersey accused me of this more than once in his memoir. I accept it. And I accept that Elder Canaan had never had such a reaction to another person—human or Rakum. He held my gaze that first time only two seconds, but I read *volumes* in that moment. Canaan looked to my escorts and listened to them introduce me. I grinned when he fought the urge to look my way. He found me goddamn gorgeous and he sent Ken and Yan off with Tork before they made note of his erection.

"Step up, asshole," he commanded when we were alone.

I wasted no time but got right into his face. If he'd have allowed it, I would have yanked him close—rough and mean—and pressed my mouth to his hard enough to bruise his lips. He read my mind and chuckled, so fucking handsome, shaking his head, his blonde curls bouncing with the move.

"You're not all that, jerkoff." He put one hand to my neck. "Show me your last assignment."

He wanted to see me with my brethren, and I thought of Elder Bel—of course, of the two of us in bed. Canaan smirked and a miniscule eye meet occurred before he wiggled his hand.

"Show me the most recent Assembly."

I was with Elder Tomás at that time and he watched

the Elder interact with me and shuffle off. Tomás did not screw ish-mikhan. *To each his own,* I thought, and Master Canaan chuckled anew.

"Boo-hoo," he said teasing and finally met my eye for longer than a moment. "Did it hurt your feelings, little brother, that Tomás would rather eat shit than spend one more second in your presence?"

Holy shit, this was it. The time had arrived for me to please my master and I felt it to my bones. I followed my muse and responded, "Yes, Master, I cry myself to sleep every sunrise."

Oh, the fire in his eyes! Shit! In a heartbeat, this amazing master drew back and brutally punched my middle as hard as he possibly could. My body flew backward with the force of it and in my torso, my organs suffered varying ruptures. I landed on the sofa, semi-longways, so as the Elder approached to resume the attack, I lifted my legs and tucked my arms up to prop my head. My internal injuries were healing and I hid my discomfort enough to say in a silky voice, "That was beautiful, Master. Please, let's do it again."

"Narcissistic asshole son of a bitch!" he barked, half-grinning and he zoomed into me, grabbing my shirt by both lapels. He jerked upward and the material frayed to nothing.

I wish you could have seen his face, holding my shirt in his hand and gazing upon my naked chest—he looked like a man drinking water in a desert. He took a deep breath and then another, his eyes scanning me slowly and with intent. He blinked once, twice, and that dashing smile hit his lips again.

"Say it," he commanded, laugh-talking.

"Master?" I asked, teasing, reclined, splayed, my mind open and so available for whatever my master wanted.

"Say it, motherfucker," he said this time in a whisper, his shoulders dropping the tiniest bit.

I needed to be careful now. I had reached the point where an ish-mikhan can err. Elder Canaan had opened himself up to abuse, to disrespect. He liked me—and this was dangerous for him. I would say the words and we'd go somewhere private. He didn't need to publicly reveal weakness of any sort—even the kind directly associated with his dick.

"Whatever I have is yours," I said low and he chuckled with relief, lowered his head, and pointed to the hallway.

With levity I rolled off the couch to land on my knees and slowly stand tall. With a flirtatious glance, I turned and left the room, his eyes on me as heavily as hands. I heard him say to Tork, *"Do not disturb."* Then I was in his bedroom. I crossed to turn and face the door, standing square, and Master Canaan walked in, slamming the door behind him.

"Darcy fucking Vandiver," he said and came toward me half the distance. "Bel favors you…"

I held his eye and stepped closer stopping five feet away. He dug around in my mind, his mental fingers jerking my thread like a mean kid pulling ponytails.

"Kilmeade favors you," he said, impressed more than before. "You are truly special."

He had said the last in a whisper and I stepped into him following my muse. The fighting was done. This Elder needed fixing and this time, I used my hands. I opened his shirt and it fell to the smooth floor and then his belt. Canaan stood quietly, his arms at his sides, watching me, half-smiling. The Elder closed his eyes to my massage and I gently pressed him to back the three strides to the bed. He allowed me to lead, respecting my vocation, and he sank onto the mattress with an exhale, as if the weight of the world had lifted from his shoulders.

Then I was lying beside him, telling him how beautiful, matchless, and perfect he was, all the while my hands, mouth, and tongue worshipped him as he deserved. Before long, he uttered a word I treasure to this day (and no one else has ever called me by this name).

"Vanny," he said, the word leaving his lungs more than simply passing his vocal chords. *"Vanny, don't ever stop."*

Shit, I love that memory.

Elder Canaan didn't send me home the next night. Elder Bel missed me and he sent for us, but Ken and Yan left without the ish-mikhan. Master Canaan held me twelve weeks and I lived more in that time than I had in the centuries before it. There is no doubt, I gave him my heart. I'm writing this memoir in 2021 and I don't sleep with my brothers these days. Yet I still think about Elder Canaan. I guess I always will.

**This delicious tale was excerpted in part from* Darcy Vandiver, Vampire Sexpert, a Memoir, *by Emil Jersey (penname)*

4

The Curse

Victoria Williams

The Curse is based upon the classic poem entitled The Lady of Shalott, second version, by Alfred, Lord Tennyson, circa 1842. It aims to not only recount the original tale, but also determine what may have happened after the poem's end. This story tells of a fair lady who lives isolated in a tower, with a mysterious curse hanging over her head which will play out if she stops her constant weaving…

The fields of barley and rye billow in the wind. As the reaper moves his scythe back and forth, he cuts each grain for harvesting, piling the sheaves together. Later they will be gathered by his strong, weathered hands and bound in large bales for storage. Working long past the hour when many had gone to bed, he hears the nightly song which floats across the water from the small island and into his ears. He pauses his reaping to listen to its haunting call, straining his eyes in the moonlight to steal a glimpse of its source: the mysterious woman rumored to live in the island tower. No one was quite sure whether she was mortal or fae, the myriad stories of her existence telling curious listeners that she had resided within the isolated tower for years, ceaselessly working and endlessly waiting.

On the island, flowers grow all around the tower, pops of yellow and white stand bold against the mossy, ancient gray stone. Within her room she sits, weaving colorful tapestries which capture the fantastical sights she sees within the mirror set against the wall. These reflections for some would be merely snippets of life from the world outside of her window, but for her, these are the entire universe.

Each day and night she sits and weaves, singing her songs as she throws the shuttle back and forth within her loom. She feels fortunate to have sight of the road that runs along the opposite riverbank. There, her view is an endless stream of townspeople, husky farmers and their wagons piled high with wares and food for sale, metal-smiths bearing wooden bars across their strong shoulders to carry cookware that glints in the sun, or young girls in their bold red cloaks headed to market with a basket in-hand.

As time goes on, some of these shadows of life become harder to bear: a couple, newly married and filled with exuberance as they head off to their life together, soldiers returning home, bloody and covered in the filth of war, their dead loaded up in wagons behind them, and bright funeral processions marching down the road towards a final resting place after the dead are prepared. Her heart aches to feel all the joys and sorrows of life, to know these people and what their lives may contain beyond their journeys down the road, and to know her own life touched theirs so deeply. It is said that if she halts her work, a curse shall be laid upon her, and although she is unsure what the curse is the fear keeps her working steadily, and her dreams faded over the years into nothing more than a forgotten memory.

One day, she views the knights as they are returning home from battle once again, triumphant and proud, with crowds gathered along the edges of the road, cheering and clapping at their success. Her eyes travel across her mirror from the high flags that reach above all who walk in the procession and to a shining night, sitting confidently upon his war-horse and leading all the others who trail behind him down the road. The large, red plumes set atop his silver helmet stand tall and unbroken, and she hears the victory bells installed along the bridle of his horse jingling from the distance. In that moment, she stops weaving in awe of the glorious sight reflected from within the surface of her mirror, at which point the shuttle launches off the loom, crashing into the mirror and shattering it.

"The curse is upon me!" she cries, and a flash of tears fueled by the sudden terror her heart is gripped with begins searing her eyes with their heat. Rising to her feet, she abandons her once-endless task, running down the curved, uneven stairs of her tower and through the large door to the blessed and unknown world outside. A shallow boat is resting on the shore by the river, and she grabs a sharp rock laying upon the ground at her feet. Approaching the small vessel, she carves her name within the wooden prow: *Lady of Shalott.* Pushing the boat into the water, she climbs within and begins to drift down the river towards the tall spires set atop the castle at Camelot, the sunset dimming the ambient light around her.

Floating down the river, her mournful song drifts out over the otherwise silent water, and it is lifted by the wind across the fields into windows of the homes nearby. She lays down within the boat, listening to the rushing of the water all around her, and allows her music to continue as she is carried toward the castle by the slow current which flows beneath her. Old and withered leaves are falling from the trees extending over the river, spiraling and twirling in the air as they drift downwards. They land within the boat and upon the water, leaving small ripples in its surface. The singing, a dirge chanted in the night, fades to silence as her eyes darken and her blood runs cold. And she sleeps, a corpse carried in its coffin upon the water, the moonlight reflecting off of her pale, ashen face.

In the pre-dawn light, her small boat drifts to the wooden dock built near the shore of the village nestled around the castle at Camelot. The villagers are up, preparing for their day, and they approach the strange craft with nervous apprehension. The crowd is filled with murmurs as they form questions and thoughts around what transpired before this moment, yet each of them is left bewildered.

Suddenly, Lancelot approaches the vessel, the townspeople parting their packed bodies so he may come to the front and see this mysterious corpse. He had seen the boat drifting down the river, the haunting scene illuminated with torches that lined the water.

"It's very unfortunate the world has lost such a woman as this," Lancelot remarks as he takes in her beauty. Long, golden tresses hang around her calm face and down alongside her flowing white dress, and he feels immense sorrow at the fact that he will never know her. But in that moment, her lifeless, overcast eyes drift slowly open, and she turns her face toward his. They each say nothing, but their eyes lock. His initial look of confusion softens under her gaze, and although no words leave his mouth, understanding grows between the two of them, and he is completely smitten.

His mind is filled with an almost-endless flood of

thoughts, each one of them for her and her alone. Lancelot knows in his heart that he must have been mistaken, as she isn't truly dead but only looked so her peaceful sleep. Her unusually ashen pallor is a unique feature of her endless beauty, and he feels immense remorse for having assumed such a thing. Extending a strong hand, she accepts his grasp, moving to standing as he guides her out of the boat. The two of them walk off, arm in arm, toward the castle, their route illuminated by torches burning on poles affixed along their path. The villagers stare after them, mouths agape, still unsure of what to make of the mysterious woman. As the couple takes their leave, the crowd looks once more to the boat with *Lady of Shalott* etched across the boat's prow.

Lancelot is lying on the bed in his room. His dark, curly hair and muscular figure are an embodiment of perfect handsomeness, a welcome respite for the eyes which now view him. He has become a cold, lifeless shell, drained of his blood which now courses through her body. The Lady sits calmly on the edge of the opposing side of the bed, her back to him, and turns her face outwards. Looking around the room, she examines the many vivid tapestries, woven webs of color which insulate the room from the frigid wind that slips through the cracks in the stone. The scenes contained within show the tales of the victorious, of the righteous, of kings sitting on thrones receiving their crowns, and enemies felled by arrows, of horses striding tall, and men bowing low. She finds in this moment that she is at peace and acknowledges how her cold heart which no longer beats will never again subject her to the pain of her sorrows.

She turns her gaze to Lancelot, looking over his still corpse and his eyes flicker open. The Lady's partner is returning to her in his new form, ready to embark upon the goal that will now be set upon him. She rises from the bed and walks to the other side, this time being the one to offer the steadying and welcoming hand. And he tenderly accepts with his own powerful grip and stands.

The pair walk together, his arm about her delicate waist as he guides her into the hall. They move quietly down the long corridor, almost as if floating, past paintings and murals, more scenes memorialized forever of men and their great deeds. Soon they come to a door which brings them to a narrow staircase, and they ascend the steps, Lancelot leading the way for his fair new companion. They move through the doorway and into a new hall, this one looking almost identical to the previous corridor. After a short walk they come to a closed door and Lancelot knocks.

"Lancelot, what is it that you need?" Galahad asks as he open the door, confusion etched across his face. He looks to the mysterious new woman, then to his fellow knight.

In that moment, Lancelot lunges at Galahad and begins to feed. His prey's screams are quickly silenced as the life is drained from his body, and he collapses into Lancelot's strong arms.

Standing in the background, a faint smile floats across the Lady's face. She leaves Lancelot to his task as she turns and walks towards the next room, filled with satisfaction at her new-found mission. Her smile grows.

5

Sister of the Weald

Matt Handle

A gothic spin on the Snow White fairy tale, this story takes place in mid-1700s England...

Sarah felt Lord Fitzmiller's eyes wander over her body as she busied herself tidying the master's bedchambers. The short black skirt of the required uniform barely covered the tops of her milky-white thighs and his gaze hungrily followed her as she fluffed the goose-down pillows and tucked in the linen sheets of the bed where he slumbered each night aside the lady of the house. At sixteen years old, Sarah was thirty years the man's junior, but she knew what he wanted. Unlike her young suitors of lesser means, Lord Fitzmiller had no intention of offering her a proposal in exchange for her innocence. He intended to take it for free. She had refused his blandishments for months now, but his increasing aggressiveness revealed the day would soon arrive where he would take her by force. Sarah's eyes teared up at the thought and she swiped at them before he took notice.

As she fluffed the last of the pillows, a solitary feather escaped the fabric and drifted lazily to the polished wooden floor landing under the edge of the bed.

"Pick that up. We wouldn't want the lady of the house to find a reason to have you whipped."

Sarah dutifully bent to retrieve the stray plumage. Before she could rise up, Fitzmiller leaned against her back, looming over her shoulder. One of his large hands ran its way up her right leg. and found its way to her undergarments where he clumsily grabbed at her flesh.

"So soft," he whispered. "Are you ready for me to make you a woman?"

Sarah gasped and sidestepped his touch, maneuvering her way around the bed and toward the door.

"I... I must complete my morning tasks, m'Lord," Sarah stuttered as she exited the room. She hurried down the hall, praying he wouldn't follow. When she reached the guest room at the far end of the house, she slipped inside and held her breath. Her heart hammered in her chest as she listened for any hint of pursuing footsteps. After what felt like forever, she exhaled and uttered a quiet sob.

Sarah didn't run across Lady Fitzmiller until later that afternoon. She was taking the hall rug to the edge of the forest where she would beat the dust from its weave, when she found the Lady sitting atop a log gazing into a hand mirror. She appeared to be worrying over the fine lines that had developed around the corners of her eyes. Sarah tried to retreat before the Lady saw her, but fallen leaves crunching underfoot gave her away.

"Where do you think you are going?" the Lady groused.

Sarah curtseyed. "Beg your pardon, m'Lady. I did not mean to disturb you. I was only bringing the rug to clean it."

"You do disturb me, Sarah. Intentional or not."

Sarah cast toward the ground.

"Well? Get on with it! Clean the rug before I decide to remove that beater from your hand and thrash you with it!"

Sarah hastily found a spot where the dust wouldn't blow toward the Lady of the House and began beating the dust and debris from the thick wool floor cover. When she was done, she saw that Lady Fitzmiller had stowed away her mirror and was watching her with intent.

"You think you are so pretty with your firm bosom and trim waist, don't you?"

Sarah was taken aback. "No, m'Lady! I don't think that at all."

"You think you can steal him from me with your youth and beauty, but you are just a peasant girl. You will never be anything more!"

"I don't know what to say, m'Lady. I would never steal anything, I swear!"

"Liar! Get out of my sight!" A tear ran down Lady Fitzmiller's face then, spoiling her rouge. "Go!"

Sarah clumsily curtseyed and scurried back to the house. Once she was safely behind the closed door of her modest servant's quarters, she threw herself onto the bed and sobbed.

It was two weeks later and Lady Fitzmiller was away for the afternoon when Lord Fitzmiller cornered Sarah in his room. Outside it stormed, winter winds threatening an early end to fall. Sarah had been enjoying the sound of the rain hammering the roof as she lit the candles on the nightstands when the door slammed shut behind her. She whirled around in fright. Lord

Fitzmiller's cheeks were flushed and he was in a state of half-dress, his waistcoat and tie missing and his shirt unbuttoned.

"m'Lord, is anything the matter?"

"Nothing we can't fix," he replied with a wolfish grin. Then he was upon her before she could move. He pinned her to the bed and tore the bodice of her uniform, partially exposing her breasts which he groped as she attempted to fight him off.

"Stop, m'Lord, please stop!" she pleaded to no avail.

Percival, the house butler, had driven Lady Fitzmiller in the carriage to her appointment so no one else was in the house to hear her scream.

Lord Fitzmiller yanked his trousers down his fleshy hips, exposing his erect manhood as he held her down with his other hand. She beat upon his face and chest, but it was no use. She was too small and he was too insistent.

Sarah cried out in revulsion as he attempted to enter her. His breath stank of wine and his incoherent mutterings in her ear of devotion and desire made her want to retch. She dug her nails into his shoulders and was about to rake them down his back when the doors burst open. Lady Fitzmiller strode into the room, fury in her eyes.

"I knew that little hussy would do whatever it took to get into my bed!" she snarled. She rushed forward and slapped Lord Fitzmiller across the face. He hurriedly rolled off Sarah and tried to adjust his clothes as his wife pulled a butcher's knife from her dress. She stabbed it downward between Sarah's breasts.

"He's mine!" she screamed, spittle flecking her lips and spraying Sarah's now pain-stricken face. "Mine!" she screamed again as she jabbed the knife into Sarah's soft belly. Blood now covered the blade and the bedsheets, but Lady Fitzmiller did not stop. She stabbed Sarah over and over until the girl was deathly still.

Lord Fitzmiller gaped in horror. He'd managed to get his trousers back on, but his shirt remained askew. "What have you done?" he whispered.

"What you made me," she hissed. "Percival brought me back due to the road being flooded. Go fetch him from the barn. We have a mess to clean up."

Lord Fitzmiller burned the sheets out back while his wife did her best to scrub the bloodstains from the mattress. Percival was tasked with disposing of the corpse. The portly butler rode one of the family mares through the forest, Sarah's body thrown over a smaller horse trailing behind. The cold rain soaked him through and through.

Once he was several miles away from the manor, Percival stopped the horses in a clearance and dismounted. His boots sunk two inches into the mud.

"Wonderful," he growled.

Percival walked over to the trailing horse and yanked a shovel from a makeshift bundle he had attached to the saddle. He wiped the rain from the brim of his hat then began to dig. He was not more than a foot deep when the shovel hit a large rock.

"Bugger," he muttered and moved the blade of the shovel six inches to the right and tried again. It was not long before the shovel clanged as it chipped away at another stone. Percival looked skyward at the dark clouds and pouring rain and scowled, "Enough of this!"

He dropped the shovel and pulled Sarah's corpse to the ground. Lord and Lady Fitzmiller had not bothered to change the poor girl's clothes. Her dark hair clung wet and tangled around her face while the rain rinsed away most of the blood from her exposed flesh.

"You deserved better, lassie." Percival placed the body in the shallow grave and gently positioned the girl's hands over her chest as if in prayer. "Rest in peace, love."

Percival shoveled the displaced mud over the corpse. He knew it wasn't much of a burial, but it would have to suffice. He was riding back to Fitzmiller Manor minutes later, cursing the bitter weather as he went.

The Fitzmillers hired a new maid within the week, a homely girl from Sheffield. No one questioned them when they explained that the old one had run off. Good help was hard to find…

It would be nice to think Mary Whick and the ladies of her coven simply chanced upon Sarah's body, but that would not be true. They were drawn by the smell. The seven of them had hunted the weald for days in search of a fresh corpse when they caught the scent of the ripening Sarah.

Low temperatures helped preserve the body, but it was still in bad shape by the time the coven entered the clearing. It was Emma who noticed Sarah's booted left foot sticking up from the mud. It was Harriet and Viv who dug up the rest.

Mary clapped her hands in delight when the body was fully extricated and lying at her feet.

"Blessed be, sisters. We beseech the Earth for the necessary instrument of our ritual and here she is! A housemaid by the look of her uniform; a victim of foul deed based on the nature of her wounds. Diana, Ada, fetch some branches to construct a sled. We must get her back by nightfall."

Maddy was the strongest of the seven so she did

most of the pulling as they made their way back to the cabin they called home. It was miles from the clearing and all the witches were tired and sore by the time they arrived.

"Midnight's but four scant hours away," Mary announced once they had delivered Sarah's corpse to the front porch and crossed the threshold into their humble forest abode. "Viv, stir the fire while Ada and Harriet peel the potatoes. We have just enough time to sup before we change for the ceremony."

The witches went about their tasks without complaint. Maddy fetched fresh wood while Diana and Emma set the table. They were accustomed to following Mary's orders and despite their weariness, each was excited about what the night held in store.

At midnight, all seven witches circled a crackling bonfire beneath the full moon. They were clad in black robes, their shiny faces hidden within the dark cowls. Mary chanted a spell. She called it up to the stars in a voice clear and bold. As she tossed reagents into a large cauldron suspended over the fire, the flames changed color from yellow to red to blue. The six other members of the coven whirled around the fire, their spindly shadows dancing among the surrounding leafless birch, elder, and oak. Sarah's corpse was tied to the largest of these trees, an oak sentinel that had watched over this wood for centuries.

The language Mary chanted wasn't English. It wasn't Gaelic or Latin either. It was something older, something ancient and forbidden. As the spell drew toward its conclusion, the wind began to rise. It howled through the clearing, blowing tree branches to and fro as the flames leapt toward the stars.

When Mary's chant ended, the fire was extinguished instantly, blanketing the clearing in darkness. The six other witches surrounding the now smoldering embers fell to the ground like rag dolls, exhausted and unconscious. Only Mary remained awake and standing. Sweat poured down her face and she trembled in anticipation as a multi-colored cloud of steam rose from the cauldron.

A single beam of moonlight shone down on the corpse bound to the tree. The head lolled lifeless, Sarah's now rotting face hidden by lank clumps of dark hair. Suddenly the corpse jolted as if struck by a bolt of lightning. Sarah's eyelids snapped open, revealing eyes that were black on black, not a hint of white sclera remaining.

The reanimated Sarah opened her mouth and croaked what might have been a scream if her voice had still been intact. She thrashed against the ropes that held her in place, struggling to be free.

"Calm yourself," Mary said in her most soothing tone of voice. She walked over to Sarah and began to untie the knots that bound the newly undead young woman. "We brought you back to our world to right wrongs, not to be a slave. These ropes were only to hold you still and upright until the spell could complete your transformation."

Mary finished untying the last of the knots. The rope fell in a heap at Sarah's feet. "In life, you may have served others but in death, you are free."

One by one, the six witches sleeping around the fire awoke. All of them approached Mary and Sarah with a look of wonder upon their gleaming faces.

"She lives!" Viv exclaimed.

"Glory, be!" Ada whispered.

"A wight!" Diana said in awe.

"This is our new sister," Mary stated as she took Sarah by the hand and led her in her first undead steps.

She gently adjusted the torn edges of the top of Sarah's dress, covering as much of the girl's nakedness as she could. "Do you remember what happened to you?" she asked.

Sarah looked at Mary with her black eyes then tilted her head inquisitively.

"You're horribly wounded," Mary explained. "You died of these wounds. Do you remember who gave them to you? Who stabbed you?"

Sarah opened her mouth and uttered another guttural moan.

Mary nodded in excitement. "You must go to him," she said. "You must right this wrong that's been committed against you. Before you can help us avenge others, you must avenge yourself. Lead us to him. Lead and we will follow!"

Mary and her coven had no way of knowing if the wight truly understood what they had asked of her. They had no guarantee the undead girl was not simply leading them aimlessly through the woods. However, Mary believed, and her sisters believed in her.

It took days, but in the end, the seven witches stood at the edge of the forest and looked upon Fitzmiller Manor with Sarah by their side. It was just after nightfall. The last rays of sunlight had edged over the horizon and the pale crescent moon lit the shape of the impressive estate across the expanse of yard.

"This is where it happened?" Mary asked.

Sarah nodded once and uttered a low hiss.

"Go to him," Mary instructed. "Destroy him. He can no longer harm you. When you're done, return to us. We are your sisters now and forever. We will take you home."

Sarah plodded across the yard, every step labored. She was a solitary shadow on a sea of gray. Her flesh was purple and rotten, her muscles atrophied and loose. Bones showed through in places, their stark whiteness reflected in the moonlight.

When she reached the front door, Sarah did not bother to knock. She banged her fists against the thick wood on its sturdy iron hinges and broke it to splinters. Lady Fitzmiller screamed from somewhere further inside the house.

"What is all this racket?" Percival called out as he rushed toward the trouble. He was still in his butler's uniform, but he had a cloth napkin folded into the collar of his shirt as if he had been caught in the middle of supper.

Sarah grabbed him by the head with both hands and twisted. His neck snapped and he crumpled to the floor dead. She stepped over the threshold and his body without a sound. She made her way through the halls until she came to the doors of the master's bedchambers. The sound of Lady Fitzmiller weeping could be heard within.

Sarah took hold of the door handles and yanked as hard as she could. The lock broke with a metallic crack. The doors fell open to reveal Lady Fitzmiller cowering on the bed in her nightgown. Lord Fitzmiller stood between the bed and the door in his own nightclothes, but with a sword in hand. Both of them gaped when they saw their intruder.

"You!" Lord Fitzmiller gasped. "How can this be?"

Sarah started forward, shuffling toward her killers with an uneven gait.

Lord Fitzmiller thrust his sword through Sarah's ribcage, impaling her on the blade. He smiled in triumph and looked into her dead black eyes. They did not register pain. They did not even look human. Lord Fitzmiller's smile faltered.

Sarah grabbed the Lord by his crotch and squeezed. She squeezed until his howl of agony was loud enough to force his wife to cover her ears. She squeezed until she felt his testicles squish into jelly. Lord Fitzmiller fell to his knees at Sarah's feet. His hands fluttered over his ruined manhood, his pants stained with blood, his face a mask of anguish.

Sarah looked to her left and right then snatched up the candle snuffer from its place atop the end table. She jammed it into the man's ear, shoving so hard it pierced his brain. His eyes rolled up into his head and he slumped to the floor.

Lady Fitzmiller screamed again as she watched her husband die. She pressed her back against the headboard as if hoping she could disappear through the wall behind her. Sarah shuffled forward. She pulled the sword from her body and let it fall to the floor with a clatter. When she reached the side of the bed, Sarah climbed atop it and crawled until she was astride Lady Fitzmiller. She had one bony knee on either side of the older woman and the tattered remains of her breasts hung in the Lady's terrified face.

"Don't," Lady Fitzmiller pleaded. "Please don't!"

Sarah took the woman's face in her hands then leaned down as if to steal a kiss. Lady Fitzmiller grimaced as Sarah opened her mouth and shrieked. The stench of death and decay on the wight's breath made her gag. Sarah looked Lady Fitzmiller in the eye and started to press on the sides of her skull. Tears streamed down Lady Fitzmiller's face and Sarah pressed harder. Blood ran from both her nostrils and Sarah pressed harder still. Lady Fitzmiller screamed. She screamed so loud the witches heard it outside. Sarah pressed until Lady Fitzmiller's skull caved in like an apple gone wormy and soft.

The room went quiet. Sarah wiped Lady Fitzmiller's blood and gore on the sheets. She got up from the bed and shuffled through the house to the remnants of the front door.

The coven of seven witches waited outside in a semi-circle around the front of the house. Six of them held burning torches. Maddy held the new maid instead, arms pinned behind her back. The girl looked petrified.

"What do you want to do with this one?" Maddy asked. "We caught her trying to run away."

Sarah waved an arm in dismissal then turned to face Mary.

Mary nodded to Maddy and the new maid was set free. The poor girl bounded away into the woods, barefoot and terrified, but unharmed.

"It's done?" Mary asked.

Sarah nodded once.

"Burn it," Mary told her sisters. "Burn it to the ground."

Mary took Sarah by the hand and led her across the yard toward the forest. Their silhouettes were two slim spindles of darkness against the orange and yellow flames that engulfed the manor behind them.

"Come, sister," Mary said as she gave Sarah's hand a squeeze. "It's time to go home." With that last sentiment, the Sisters of the Weald melted into the forest, their newest member in hand.

6

Silent Justice

Faye Brooks

It happened so fast...
But now he'll pay.

I heard him slam into the house, loud and bullying – as always.

I was with her in the kitchen when he charged in, and I quickly hid. He didn't even look at me; he rarely notices me at all, except to yell at and shove aside. I'm always in the way; small as I am, I'm still in his way.

I heard him, and hid before he could kick me aside.

I hid and watched... and listened...

To his shouting, cursing, and threats.

To her screams, of anger...

Then fear...

Then pain...

I watched, as light glinted on sharp, shiny metal.

I watched, as she cried out once, twice... then she fell.

Silence.

He looked around, breathing hard, eyes burning with rage, and hatred, and fear.

I hid.

He looked at the cellar door.

He picked her up, staggered a bit under her dead weight, and stumbled across the kitchen. Grunting, he shifted her weight, and lurched toward the door to the cellar. He nearly dropped her as he turned the knob and kicked the door inward..

I watched, anger growing within me.

I watched, anger becoming vengeance.

I watched, vengeance becoming action.

He would pay...

He fumbled for the light switch, and I jumped out; although small, I am fast, and agile, and vengeful.

He would pay... Now!

He gave a short, startled cry, and toppled down the long, steep flight of wooden steps, crashing with a solid THUD! CRACK! *on the concrete floor of the basement.*

Silence.

Again.

Complete, this time.

But I am still sad, for I loved her, and will miss her...

"Hey, Harry, down here!" Officer Joe Dawson called from the lower steps. "Found the problem!"

Officer Harry Grayson paused at the small landing, grimacing with distaste. "Jeezzz, what a stench! No wonder the neighbor was complaining."

"Yeah. Both dead; looks like he stabbed her, then fell down the stairs when he tried to carry her down to the basement." Dawson bent over the bodies carefully, touching them only to check for a pulse.

Grayson remained at the doorway off the small kitchen. "Sometimes, things work out right."

"Yep. Had to be an accident," Dawson commented, joining his partner at the landing. "'Cause ain't no one or nothing around except that big ol' Tabby there in the kitchen."

EPILOG

I have a new home now; a new life. My old life is gone, but not forgotten.

And I will watch over my charge, and keep her from harm.

I love her already.

The bigger one with the deep voice better treat her right.

I'm small, yet I am vengeful.

I am justice.

7

Haunted Ghosts

Faye Brooks

Houses aren't the only things haunted by ghosts.

The white, late model Ford van, nearly undistinguishable from the six-foot snow drifts, skewed in a slight skid as it stopped before large, ornate double doors of a multi-storied, turreted and gabled Victorian mansion.

Gossman Manor stood cold and proud before them, shunning all aspects of modern, Twentieth-Century mores and means. Its forbidding towers and turrets distained any welcoming attitude, the floor-to-ceiling windows glaring at the world through dark, dismal panes. Much like its builder: Matthew Jonathan Gossman.

Undaunted by the less-than-appealing aspects of the house, the driver, one Madame Minerva Milligan, renown Psychic to the Stars and Ghost Investigator, waved cheerily at her passengers. "Here we are, folks. Bundle up, it's cold outside, and that old house is probably drafty as hell."

Front doors and sliding doors opened, expelling five like-minded psychic researchers into the wintry mix of sleet and snow. Staring at the foreboding edifice, they waited in silence until Madame Minerva addressed them.

"Now," she said, gusts of fog accenting each word, "Ladies and gents, I need to warn you that Mr. Gossman is… well… a bit off-putting. Just ignore his eccentric nature; he did, after all, agree to allow us to have our Gathering at his home."

"Is he always difficult?" Amelia, the youngest and newest member of the group, spoke up.

"Yes. But he's basically harmless. All bark and no bite."

"Then why did he agree to these Gatherings?"

"Look around you, dear," she waved an arm around the vast estate, a frozen Artic tableau of icicle-laden topiaries and trees, bordered by frosted gardens. "This mausoleum is miles from civilization; he won't admit it, but he must be lonely. The upkeep on this place must be staggering – not to mention the taxes…

"But whatever his reasons, Mr. Gossman has never been a disappointment. Disrupting, maybe, but never disappointing."

"Stuff and nonsense, I tell you," Gossman muttered, annoyed. "I keep telling you people: *There. Are. No. Ghosts.*"

He glared at the group arranged around the table, holding hands, chanting inanely, going into trances – foolish chicanery. Bad enough he had allowed them to set up God-knew-what ridiculous equipment throughout the lower floor (a 'ghost sensor' in every room), but now they insisted in talking to non-existent spirits. Foolish people willing to believe a self-proclaimed medium, wanting answers to assuage their guilty consciences…

It was enough to drive any ghost *away*, instead of enticing them in.

"Now, now, Mr. Gossman," Madame Minerva admonished. "Be good. You know what we do and what to expect. Are you going to comply, or should we come back later?"

"Oh, go on, you old fake. You'd think these idiots would be onto you by now."

Madame Minerva smiled reassuringly at the bemused group, then turned her attention back to their host. "Do you know why the house is haunted, Mr. Gossman?"

"I told you, you damned gypsy, it *isn't* haunted!"

"Oh, but it is. There are ghosts everywhere." She nodded to Amelia, "You sense them, don't you, dear?'

"Oh, yes! I sense them; they are here, in the house. They are… annoyed, I think."

The oldest of the group, Adam York, raised his hand meekly. "I do, too. Several of them. I … do not want to disturb them."

"And the rest of you?"

The remaining three looked at each other, then replied, "Yes," in nervous voices. Then remained silent.

"You see, Mr. Gossman, you just don't want to admit it. You'd be much better off, and much more amiable, if you'll just accept that."

"Pure balderdash! I won't abide anymore of this garbage! Leave your money and get out of my house! Don't come back!"

"I apologize for Mr. Gossman's outburst. He's in an ornery mood today. Our Gatherings usually last longer than this. But, it is his house, and we have to leave when he tells us to."

Gossman watched as the van slid out of the curved drive into the ice-laden street. Letting the heavy drapes fall back into place, he called out, "You can come out now."

"Have they left?" An elderly woman, well into her eighties, drifted in; her diaphanous dressing gown floating like a white cloud, the lacy ruffle fading out a foot above the floor. Several shadowy, transparent forms followed her into the parlor, where the séance had taken place.

"Yes. Finally."

"Why do you keep allowing them to come here?" A middle-aged man, dressed in military attire from a long-ago war, settled on an overstuffed chair. His form grew transparent from the knees down. "It's the same silly thing, over and over. And those … machines… are very annoying."

"I know. But they are too stupid to know -- or admit – that they died in a highway accident five years ago after leaving this house."

"What do we do about the bunch in the Dining Room?"

"Ignore them, and they'll eventually leave."

Professor Carstairs of the Psychic Investigation Department of Loyola State U, removed his ectoplasmic visor and beamed at his students. "See, even ghosts have ghosts…"

Bullets and Blood

Chris Snider

The year was 1883 as Ryan Redfield and his gang of bank robbers had just eluded the posse that chased them from a large Texas town. They now headed South for the Mexican border to escape justice and spend the 50,000 dollars they had stolen, splitting it five ways. It was dusk by the time they stopped to catch their breath.

"WHOOOO HOOO!" Ryan shouted. "Damn, that was a perfect job! How sweet it was to put two bullets in the gut of that old son of a bitch sheriff that always looked at me like I was shit he wiped off his shoe."

Ryan was a handsome devil with a grin that drove girls wild. His blonde hair was a mess and his beard needed trimming, but all the ladies found him desirable.

"Fifty grand," Joey Logan said shaking his head in disbelief. "I know the Good Lord isn't on our side, but it was a miracle we pulled this off with none of us taking one bullet."

"That was due to the new kid," Ryan said looking at a young shy half-Mexican named Antonio Angelos. "I thought I was a quick draw, but you're quicker than lightning, kid."

The kid had been with the gang only a week and he turned out to be a great addition.

"I think we lost them," Carlos Perez, the full-blooded Mexican of the gang said looking behind them. "We still need to keep moving, though. Either that or find a place to hole up until tomorrow."

"Might be a good idea," Ryan agreed. "The border is still a good day and a half ride from here."

"This place is a damn desert," Luke Hayes, the fifth member of the group said. "Where we going to find a hiding hole?"

"I know a place," Antonio said. "It's about fifteen miles to the west. It's pretty much a ghost town by now but we could hole up there."

"He hasn't led us wrong yet," Ryan said addressing the gang. "Let's do it."

It took a little over two hours for them to arrive at the town once called "Hell's Range." The five of them and especially their horses were exhausted. Most of the town was visible as the night was clear and the stars were shining down bright.

"Not exactly an inviting town name, is it?" Carlos asked crossing himself despite his career choice.

"No," Ryan agreed, "but that's not my worry right now. We have to get these horses some water fast. We've rode them hard since the hold up and with this heat, they might keel over. That happens, we're screwed."

"That's a fact," Joey declared. "I plan on getting to Mexico with this money and getting me a pretty little senorita."

"Just one?" Ryan chuckled. "That first night I plan on having at LEAST two in my bed." This brought a laugh to the whole gang, helping them wind down from the events of the day.

Ryan pulled out the bag of money and just *looked* at it. The five of them could live like kings in Mexico with their shares. After all these years things were finally going his way. Then, out of the corner of his eye he saw someone coming out of the old Saloon. Ryan turned his head to see a woman in a red corset (with a *very* endowed chest) walking toward them. She had curly blonde hair and green eyes the color of jade. Her mouth formed a seductive grin as she neared.

"I guess this isn't as much of a ghost town as we thought," Carlos mumbled with his eyes on the girl.

She put her arms around Luke and got within a whisker of his lips before saying, "You cowboys look tired. How about a drink and a ride from something besides a horse?"

"Did we really die and go to heaven?" Luke said.

"Kind of doubt heaven is where we would have ended up," Ryan said eyeing the girl suspiciously.

A door opened to Ryan's left and two men walked out of the general store. One was bald with a gray goatee, the other was clean shaven and had his long blonde hair tied back in a ponytail.

"Not very often we get visitors, is it Duke?" the bald one said.

"No, it's not, John."

"What do you reckon is in that sack he's holding?"

"Well, I'm no educated man, but I think these five look like bank robbers and that's likely a sack with a shit-ton of money inside."

"Well, now, ain't that exciting?"

Joey hopped down off his horse and said, "We

don't want no trouble, mister."

The two strangers continued as if they didn't even hear.

"I've got an idea, John."

"What's that?"

"How about we kill these guys and take that money for ourselves?"

"That's a right smart idea, Duke."

Ryan furrowed his brow. They were five armed robbers and these two appeared unarmed. Were they brave or just plain stupid?

The strangers walked forward but Joey pulled out his Bowie knife and buried it in the gut of the one named Duke, spilling his guts to the dirt road. Ryan drew his Colt Peacemaker and shot John in the chest three times.

"Well, that was stupid," Carlos said.

Ryan had an uneasy feeling. He noticed that the girl clinging to Luke didn't even so much as yelp at the violence, her demeanor as calm as before.

"Are there any more crazies hiding here?" Carlos asked still on his horse.

Ryan's uneasiness evolved to downright fear as the two people they just killed begin to stir. Slowly they sat up and then stood. The gang watched in wide-eyed awe as the hole in Duke's belly and John's three bullet wounds healed.

"Well, shit…" Ryan said. "Didn't see that coming."

"El Diablo!" Carlos whispered.

Without warning, the strangers then launched onto Joey, each taking a side of his neck and ripping it out. They turned to the remaining four, revealing elongated fangs dripping blood. The horses bolted in terror, flipping Carlos off the back of his mount as it left the circle. In the next second the woman sank her teeth into Luke, tearing his neck out and hissing as her counterparts had moments earlier.

Even though he knew it wouldn't do much good, Ryan emptied his second pistol into the two men. Carlos pulled his Winchester and put four slugs into the woman.

"Get to the saloon!" Ryan shouted.

"What if there's more inside?!" Antonio barked.

"We're dead either way," Ryan answered. "We try to run, they'll chase us down."

The remaining gang members backed into the saloon. The three demons were down and bleeding, but healing quick.

"Holy hell!" Ryan said. "Vampires! That has to be what they are."

"I thought they were just campfire stories!" Carlos said.

"They look pretty damn real to me, Carlos!"

"Maybe coming here was a bad idea," Antonio said.

"Ya think?! No use dwelling on it, let's just try to stay alive. Sunlight kills them, right? The sun's only been down about three hours. What else kills vampires?"

"Stake through the heart," Carlos offered.

"We don't have that either."

"No, but we can sure as hell make some." Ryan broke the legs off a chair, tossing one a piece to Carlos and Antonio. "Get your knives out and start sharpening. We can send those blood suckers back to hell."

After a couple of minutes, they had their new weapons ready. Ryan walked to a window and his heart dropped. The three they had incapacitated were up and had been joined by at least five more of their ilk, huddling in a demon's meeting. The one called John said something to two of the others and pointed to the side of the building. Ryan gasped as the two of them turned into bats and flew toward the saloon.

"Carlos! Antonio! Go to that side room and see if there are any doors or windows! They're going to try to flank us!"

Carlos and Antonio did as ordered and disappeared through the side door. Ryan braced himself and waited to see if anyone would come straight at him for a fight. He was watching the door but was startled as the saloon girl came crashing through the window. She smiled and shined her fangs.

"What's the matter, baby? Don't you think I'm pretty? Spend a little time with me. You don't want to hurt my feelings, do you?"

"I personally prefer my bed buddies not to be possessed by the devil."

She hissed and launched at him sending him flying over the bar. Ryan's body crashed into multiple bottles of booze fell to the floor. She walked over still smiling, not taking him for a threat. Reaching over the bar, she lifted him up by the hair. Ryan brought an unbroken bottle with him and busted it over her head, causing her to shriek more in annoyance than pain. Then he shoved the jagged remains of glass into her forehead.

While she was busy trying to remove it, Ryan took the homemade stake and shoved it through her heart. She wailed and her skin melted off before the bones turned to dust.

Glass shattered and Carlos screamed in the other room. Ryan leaped over the bar and ran to be of any help. Unfortunately, he was too late. A huge white wolf (which he assumed was another form of the demons) was eating away at Carlos's throat.

There was no sign of Antonio. He must have been taken away to be ripped to shreds. Ryan was all alone. In a matter of minutes, he had gone from the leader of a five-man gang to the soul survivor fighting for his life.

When he walked back out, two unknown vampires had just come through the door. Ryan ran up the stairs for higher ground. He went down a hall to the left and entered a room, slamming and locking the door.

He had trapped himself, yes, but at least there was only one narrow direction they could come at him from, maybe giving him a fighting chance. Ryan heard heavy footfalls coming his way. The lock on the door did little good as a clawed fist busted through. Not bothering to unlock it, the vampire tore it off its hinges. The one with the stringy blonde hair charged at Ryan and punched him with what felt like the strength of five men. It straddled Ryan, gripping head, and brought its teeth toward his neck. Ryan had to use his left hand to hold it back, but brought up the stake with his right to destroy it.

By the time Ryan stood up, the other one, with black hair and a beard, was charging him and pinned him against the wall. It went for his neck and Ryan dropped the stake to have both hands free to fend the thing off. After a short struggle, Ryan head-butted it, likely doing more damage to himself, and kicked it in the crotch. The vampire curled its middle. This apparently was one thing that affected males the same way whether they be mortal or undead.

Ryan grabbed the stake and stood there daring his opponent to come forward. But he had made a critical miscalculation. There was a window behind him and these monsters could reach it. He did not have time to react—he was out.

Ryan opened his eyes to the hazy image of a room full of vampires, more than he saw before. He was being held by two of them, John and Duke. He soon realized they were still in the Saloon, but he had been brought back to the bottom floor.

He watched the same white wolf that had done in Carlos come in through the door with blood staining its mouth. It took the form of a man, but not just any man. It was Antonio.

"What the hell???"

"I knew you were a tough one, Ryan."

"No way! You can't be one of them! I saw you walking around in broad damn daylight! You couldn't be a vampire!"

"That is the case for most vampires, but like I'm only half-Mexican, I'm only half vampire. My daddy was a bit of a horndog who liked bedding any woman he could. He ended up knocking up my mother and I was born nine months later, a half breed in more than one sense. Not the first time that ever happened, but I got the VERY rare quality of being able to walk in the sunlight."

"Why all of this, then?"

"I had been watching you and your gang for a while. I was a bat flying overhead or a wolf in the distance, and I knew you guys were about to pull off that bank job."

"That's why you conveniently showed up one week before to join us. That's also why you were such a quick draw."

"Now you're catching on."

"So this whole thing was just about getting the money? What the hell did you need us for? You all could have robbed the bank yourselves."

"Now, that wouldn't be very smart, would it? Supernatural creatures showing up in towns, slaughtering people, and making ourselves known? While there are a good many of us, we're still outnumbered by humans. We like to keep our little society secret, so you can imagine how valuable I am to the community being able to go anywhere I want at any time."

"You used us to pull the bank job and led us here to take the money."

"Well, the money is part of it, so I can go around different places buying up the things we need, but there was one other thing. Notice how you're still alive?"

"Why is that?"

"We don't turn just anybody into a vampire. While it does make you more powerful, weak humans make weak vampires and strong humans make strong vampires. You're a strong human. I sensed that the first time I saw you. Joey, Luke, and Carlos were average, so they didn't make the cut. You, however, did. You will be a great asset to us."

"Shit," was all Ryan could say.

"I've grown fond of you, Ryan. Time to make you one of the army of the night."

This was it. There was no escaping and even if he could there was no getting away. Ryan only said one more thing before Antonio sank his fangs into his neck.

"I really wish I had gone with my Mama to church more…"

Ovenia, Wizard's Apprentice

Katie Barnett

A stray red curl drifted into Ovenia's eyes as she stood with her parents and siblings waiting with the rest of the working-class families. She had just turned ten and Lord Hurst called his serfs to assemble in the central bailey. Warrik, the sorcerer, would be selecting an apprentice that day.

As the sorcerer moved through the crowd, many of the serfs grew nervous and some even backed away. When he walked to where Ovenia and her parents stood, he closed his eyes and held out his hands, palms horizontal to the ground. The air shivered in a bubble around them and Ovenia's parents tucked her closer between them.

Warrik opened his eyes and knelt to one knee. "What is the name of the child?"

"Ovenia," her father answered.

"And her age?"

"This is her tenth year."

Warrik nodded. "I will call her to my service and treat her kindly." Then he looked to Ovenia's mother. "And you know already she is blessed by the Earth?"

Witchcraft ran through the women in her line and indeed, Ovenia possessed the same talent. "Yes, she is."

Warrick stood with a single nod. "Your family will be called to my service so you may stay with the child. Go. Pack your household. From this day, you will live as part of my staff in the castle wing Lord Hurst has provided me."

It had been a blessing to leave their one-room thatch-roofed house and move into the two furnished rooms Warrik assigned. The blessings continued as Ovenia gained Warrik's favor. He arranged for her father to become one of Lord Hurst personal staff. Her younger siblings were taught by the castle's tutor. One brother had begun training with the Lord's private secretary. Ovenia's position as apprentice benefited them all.

Warrik spent the first few years working on Ovenia's basic education before she started spell crafting or potion brewing. By the time Ovenia was thirteen, she was well-read, quick-witted, and bold. Daily, she pushed Warrik to teach her more about magic and less about history. Impatient as any youth, her frustration grew. One night, she entered Warrik's workroom after he had gone to bed.

The large spell-book which always sat on his desk caught her eye. The quill stuck out of it, marking his place. This writing utensil was white with gray flecks on either side of the shaft. When she lifted the quill a swirl of energy raced up her arm. Warrik's magic hummed within, trapped, preserved, as if stored from years of being held as his powers flowed through him. Her eyes shone with excitement as she turned to his notes on a conjure to stir the air. Into the night, she focused her energy into executing the spell.

Warrik realized she was in his workroom as soon as

she touched the quill, her action causing his magic to shift and he watched from the shadows. It took some time, but finally, the air jerked into motion. It whirled, tossing papers and dried herbs from their resting places. She lifted her arms in exhilaration and her red curls whipped around her like a victorious banner. Then she realized she did not know the counter-curse. She turned to the spell-book frantically flipping through the thick papyrus, but the whirling wind made it difficult to keep the book on a certain page and prevent her wild hair from whipping across her eyes. When Warrik laughed at her predicament, she startled and dropped the book onto the table. The wizard stepped out of the shadows still laughing. Ovenia assumed a contrite expression and apologized, but even that was difficult with the wind blowing her hair repeatedly into her mouth.

He continued his amusement and Ovenia huffed with a glare to her master. "Stop your laughing and help me!" But as he chortled, a grin broke across her own lips and she joined his laughter.

The wind continued to knock everything into chaos as the two of them stood side by side and laughed. Finally, Warrik lifted both hands and spoke the counter-spell through a laugh and the air fell still. He opened a drawer and withdrew a spell-book and handed it to Ovenia, along with a pure white feather quill. "You are ready. I will teach you the spells that will fill it up."

Ovenia hugged it against her chest with joy. Then she leapt the distance between them and hugged him, too. Warrik placed his hands on her head and kissed the top of those riotous red curls.

From that day, he trained her in the spell-casting arts. Her talents matched his own by her seventeenth year and Warrick said she would surely one day surpass him. However, this burgeoning power did not go unnoticed. Lady Hurst, wife of Ovenia's overlord, learned of the serf girl whose power would rival that of the wizard's experience and wisdom. She was of an unkind nature, possessing such extreme vanity that she could not tolerate another woman in her home who may be regarded as fairer or more charming than she.

One evening, Warrik returned from a meeting with Lord Hurst and entered the workroom with a heavy heart. Ovenia glanced up from her studies to meet him with a smile that faltered when she noticed his wilted demeanor.

"What has happened this day?" she asked with alarm.

"Ovenia, my dear child, our time together has come to an end."

The swirl of her red curls was immediate as she shook her head. "That cannot be. I have much more to learn. You mustn't depart from me this soon."

He sighed and stroked his thick fingers through the white whiskers on his jaw. "Lord and Lady Hurst have removed you from your apprenticeship, finding it unseemly for a woman of your age to neglect learning the feminine arts. You will be Lady Hurst's personal maid."

Ovenia's eyes grew as outrage transformed her features. When she spoke, it was with a strained whisper. "She would have me set aside the blessings of my magic to brush her hair and remove her stockings?"

The skin of Ovenia's neck grew as red as her hair as her anger simmered. In their time together, Warrik had carefully interceded when her rebellious heart overrode a chance for calm thought. But now, he was equally frustrated and did not rebuke her strong response.

"I know it is a waste, my child, but I would not have the rest of your family suffer for my or your refusal to obey the masters' bidding."

A break of breath stole across her lips in wordless frustration; he was right. She would do what they wilt so her parents and siblings could retain their positions of favor. So, Ovenia gathered her belongings and left the workroom, and Warrik, behind.

Lady Hurst sat before her vanity mirror having her hair styled when Ovenia entered her room a short time later. The woman met her gaze in the reflection and disapproval filled her eyes. Ovenia had become a strikingly attractive young lady and Lady Hurst was not pleased.

"You will not wear your hair unbound in this house," she snapped.

It had not occurred to Ovenia to do anything special with her appearance and she frowned. "Oh, my Lady, I apologize."

Lady Hurst looked to the maid doing her hair. "Get a head covering for that servant and see that it is fitted properly."

Ovenia was pulled further into the room and given a seat while the maid began tucking her hair into a plain brown cloth covering. Lady Hurst sneered down her nose at her and returned to her mirror.

She opened a jar of face cream. "After all," she smirked, "we must present our best to the King tonight."

"I am to meet the King?" Ovenia asked with wonder.

Lady Hurst burst into a condescending laugh. "Absolutely not! You are much too unkempt to deserve the presence of the King. You will remain unseen."

Ovenia dug her fingernails into her own palms to

squelch her response. But her frustration would not be completely contained. Magic weaved into her thoughts and intentions as she silently applied an enchantment to the cream Lady Hurst dipped her fingers into. She willed purpose into that jar that it not soothe and soften the face to which it was applied, but instead, reveal the ugliness of the woman's heart on her face. Ovenia binded the spell as Lady Hurst swept the first layer of cream across her cheeks.

The maid finished tucking Ovenia's hair into the ugly covering and Lady Hurst sneered at her as she continued to apply the face cream.

"Now, girl, go work my flower garden since you are not yet trained to dress me for royal presentation. I will rest before the King's arrival."

Ovenia stood from her seat without a word and left the Lady's chambers. She went and worked in the gardens as she was bid. It was several hours later, when Ovenia was hot and dirty from weeding and pruning, that the King and his entourage arrived.

When the maid woke Lady Hurst from her nap, she gasped at what she saw. Dark circles rimmed her eyes, her skin had turned a sickly pale and spots marred her previously pristine complexion. Wrinkles snaked the corners of her mouth and wriggled across her forehead. None of the beauty that Lady Hurst had been so boastful of remained. Ovenia heard her shriek from where she stood among the rose bushes.

The young King was named Edward and quite handsome. He was well loved by his court and subjects. He greeted Lord Hurst with warmth before seeing to the comfort of the ones that traveled with him. One of those was his twelve-year-old niece. They were in this part of the country to collect her and bring her to his palace for the social season. His niece, Katherine, strolled into the gardens where Ovenia worked. She had preferred to ride her own horse for the journey to the Hurst's castle and had taken several detours off the road to wade through creeks or explore forest trails. Between that and the dirt kicked up by the carriages and wagons in the processional, his niece did not look like much of a princess. Her dress was torn and she covered in a fair amount of dirt. Katherine hopped upon one of the low garden walls and began to tightrope-walk down it. A moment later, she took a tumble.

King Edward noticed and rushed out to help her, but paused when he realized Ovenia had already arrived to her side. The serf girl was pretty despite the rag covering her hair. She smiled at Katherine and soothed her tears, cleaning off her scraped arm and knee. Edward remained concealed behind the archway of the nearby entrance as Ovenia had Katherine close her eyes and count to twenty. As her eyes were closed, Edward watched Ovenia whisper a spell and hold her hand over the scrapes. The skin healed before Katherine finished counting.

Edward found himself in awe of this serf girl because the injuries had not been severe and it was sometimes a risk for a woman to use magic in the open. Wizards were accepted as men, but sometimes women were branded as witches and persecuted. He was sure the girl had no clue she had just performed this service for a princess.

Katherine thanked Ovenia and said her goodbyes. She ran to the entry door finding her Uncle standing there as she stepped through.

"Did you see the lady wizard fix me? She thought she kept it a secret, but I peeked."

He smiled at her. "I did. Think I should go say hi?"

"Oh yes, she's ever so nice."

Katherine's nanny found them then and took the princess upstairs to be cleaned up.

Later in the large assembly, all in the dining hall were beginning to enjoy themselves. Edward glanced at his people but still wanted to personally thank the serf girl from the garden. He slipped out and returned to the garden. At that moment, Lady Hurst rushed past him not noticing who he was. He watched unseen as she gripped Ovenia's arm and jerked her aside.

"I know of your powers, girl! Use them to restore my beauty!"

"My Lady, Warrik assured me that you do not approve of my studies in his magical craft. I dare not go against your approval."

"Stupid girl! Use your unnatural powers and restore my beauty or your family will be put out with a boot to the arse!"

The King noted the pain flicker across Ovenia's face. She then yanked the covering from her hair, her red curls spilling down her back in a fiery river. Lady Hurst started to object but stopped as Ovenia raised her hand and held it over the Lady's face. The wind swept around them as her magic arose, bringing with it an intense scent of flowers. Then, the enchantment lifted from Lady Hurst's face and dissipated on the wind. Her beauty restored, Lady Hurst gave a contented sigh before again glaring at Ovenia.

"Go back to your bed for the night and be ready to work at sunrise."

The King ducked around the corner as Lady Hurst returned to the house. He heard Ovenia muttering as she gathered her gardening tools and he went out to meet her.

"Hello, magical maiden," he greeted as he approached.

Startled, Ovenia whirled and met his gaze. She dropped into a deep curtsey once she spotted his crown. "Your Majesty, I am honored."

"Why are you working the flowers if you are talented in the magical arts?"

"It is what my Lady bid me to do."

"Well, I shall speak to Lord Hurst about this. Someone of your talent would be better used for other things. You performed a service for your Lady and that should be rewarded."

He turned but stopped when Ovenia burst out, "Wait!"

"Yes?"

A blush crept across her cheeks as she dropped her gaze. "Please do not."

"Why not?"

"I do not deserve it," she replied in a soft tone.

"I do not understand," the King responded.

Ovenia inhaled deep, clasping her hands before her. "It was I who caused the mishap of her face."

"Oh? Why?"

Ovenia released a child-like huff that amused the King, although he hid his response.

"The Lady can be unkind," Ovenia managed in a whisper.

"Ah, perhaps telling you to wear that ugly head covering and sending you to bed without meeting the King?"

"Yes!" Ovenia replied with fire, then caught herself and schooled her features to be more demure. "Yes, my King."

Suddenly, Warrik appeared beside her and placed a protective hand to her shoulder. He bowed to the king. "Your Majesty," he implored, "please forgive my apprentice for her actions. I was also angry that they ended her time with me; I am the one to be held accountable for Ovenia's frustration."

The King held up his hand. "Sir Wizard, there is no need for apology or explanation." He moved closer and took Ovenia's hand, raising it up to his lips. "My name is Edward."

Her hand was so small in his and his kind eyes so intent as he looked at her that Ovenia forgot how to breathe. "I am Ovenia."

His lips brushed across her knuckles and Ovenia questioned whether her knees would continue to hold her upright.

"Ovenia, I saw how Lady Hurst treated you. I also saw how you healed my niece after she fell from the garden wall." Edward released her hand and stood upright, reaching over to shake Warrik's hand. "My court does not have a wizard. Are you and your apprentice available to relocate to my palace to continue your work there?" Warrik and Ovenia gave him a moment of stunned silence. The King looked back to Ovenia and smiled, "Of course, this would include any family members as well."

"Yes!" she blurted out, then covered her mouth with her hand and sending her wizard mentor a sheepish look.

Warrik laughed, hugging her up against his side. "Immediately, my Lord! We will leave with you when you go."

Edward nodded, gave Ovenia a lingering glance, and then returned to the Hall before people began to look for him. Warrik cupped Ovenia's face in his hands and looked upon her with pride. Then they both went to prepare themselves for the journey and for Ovenia to tell her family her happy news.

The dust drifted in the air as she packed her things. She turned to Warrik's desk and lifted his old white and grey feathered quill off his spell-book. His energy washed across her like a warm breath just as it had the first night she had touched it, the night she first stirred the air. She held it to her chest and let out a shuttered breath, happy that Warrik had chosen her.

Warrik walked through the door. "I think it is time for that quill to belong to you, child."

"I cannot, you still have much use for it."

"It is a gift," he replied, "Because you have been a gift to me."

She hugged him tight, emotions clouding her vision with tears. They finished packing and she paused before she walked out, looking around at that so-familiar workroom where she had spent hours of her youth. There were too many fond memories to count.

Ovenia left that well-loved workroom with her master's quill in hand, stepping into a new life of possibilities. There would be many more years to learn all that Warrik had to teach her, her family would be well taken care of, and a kind young King might have already fallen under her spell. The sorceress tucked one stray red curl behind her ear and smiled.

10

Brothel Lessons

DH Lee & Emil Stern

Year 1745

Born to an ancient vampire race, Darcy Vandiver enjoyed his charmed life to the fullest. By age nine, his teachers recognized his specialty – he was "ish-mikhan" – one born with the rare ability to "fix" anyone's sexual frustrations. On the evening of Darcy's thirtieth year, the master began sending him to brothels to practice his technique.

"The boy! I want the boy!"

The sentiment echoed in Darcy's mind, spoken by every man and woman seeking physical attention. The brothel owner served the Rakum and therefore, allowed Darcy to make the choice. Oh, the fun of turning the tables on the stupid blood-bags each expecting only carnal fulfillment.

"Line them up," Darcy whispered to the keeper as eleven mortal patrons argued over who would buy time with the beautiful boy with the long, cinnamon hair. He appeared barely fourteen to human eyes but was tall—over six feet and still growing. Adonis and Master Pebb had been diligently developing his musculature, so he was strapping, balanced head-to-toe with muscle, his adolescent shoulders round and thick. When the patrons heard Herr Ingle's instructions, each one turned angry words and threats his direction.

"Line up or exit," the keeper told them in an even tone, not cowed. "This boy is special; you can all see it. Line up; he will choose his companions."

Still cursing, one-by-one, the patrons shuffled to the wall in a loose firing line, eyes seeking Darcy's. He stood in the center watching them assemble. None of them were attractive, none smelled clean, and Darcy found none of them appealing.

So… how to choose, he mused. Tonight's lesson was about manipulating and controlling mortals; there would be no need to undress or even touch them, except to draw the winner's blood.

What criteria would most please Master Pebb? Strength and size.

Darcy eyed the line-up left to right. Then his mouth formed a small grin. "That one," he said low and met the bloated tick's eye.

A rumble of frustration filled the room as the keeper ushered the unchosen to the next room where the hired prostitutes waited. The one Darcy had chosen remained, grinning and wringing his cap in his dirty and callused hands. Herr Ingle stepped close enough to the blob to receive his coins and then turned for the rooms.

With a questioning pause, the mortal watched Darcy, unsure if he should lead or follow. Darcy held a fathomless gaze which the man deciphered to mean he should go first. Once he waddled behind the brothel keeper, Darcy brought up the rear. He always kept them in front—never trust a mortal to stand behind you—one of Master Pebb's more recent lessons.

On a similar learning experience, the master brought Darcy and Adonis to a rowdy drinking establishment. Whomever Adonis chose, Darcy was to overcome. His proctor called it, "smash, fuck, drink, and strangle." In their language, *Jus, polt, va'* and *gyu*, the anacronym—*Jolvag*—formed the Rakum word for "laugh." This tickled their master and the night in question, he sent his servants in for a "laugh" that he would experience vicariously from the castle. *"Never let a mortal stand behind you,"* came into play when the man Adonis picked out stabbed Darcy in the back, driving his hunting blade four inches deep. Adonis ended the mortal in a heartbeat but was forced to carry Darcy to the carriage bleeding and mostly unconscious. When they returned to the master, Pebb healed his ish-mikhan's wounds, but didn't let him forget how his carelessness ruined a perfectly well-laid evening. Tonight, again his master expected diversion, and Darcy would make certain everything transpired as planned.

The brothel keeper pushed open a door at the end of the south hallway and stepped well back. Was he shying from Darcy? Probably. Ingle was a Cow, but his master was a Rakum named Oman whom Darcy had seen strike Ingle with an open hand on several occasions.

I'm not going to hit you, Darcy said internally, of course, not to the man, but he did stop in his face. Ingle's eyebrows went up and he leaned back.

"Anything else, Master?" he whispered so the patron wouldn't hear. "Is this okay?"

Darcy lowered his chin and batted his lashes, aware he was perceived as a harmless child to his chosen lout, but this Cow knew better. Darcy brought up his hand to touch Ingle's cheek, slowly so as not to frighten him further.

"I'm a friend, Herr Ingle," Darcy said in a quiet tone and held the man's gaze. Ingle was Darcy's height and although fifty-two, he remained strong and healthy in a village where many men died before that mark. "I like your face, but not your expression. When our eyes meet, I want to see joy, an eagerness to see me happy." Darcy stepped into his space and tenderly cupped his cheeks with both hands. "Do you want to see me happy?"

"Yes, Master," Ingle replied breathless.

Darcy leaned close and allowed his lips to barely touch Ingle's cheek, then he remained there, his breathing feathering on the man's ruddy jaw. "If I were to kiss you, would your expression change? Would I see in your eyes affection and allegiance?"

Darcy had whispered against the man's ear and Ingle held his breath, his heart beating faster than ever. With a small movement, an inch to his right and Darcy touched his lips to Ingle's, not pressing the kiss in, but waiting for the man to exhale. In less than three seconds, Ingle did, and Darcy pressed in, sealing their connection so the mortal's breath released entirely into Darcy. When he pulled back, he licked his lips and remained close, looking the man in the face and feeling his full-blown arousal in the contact their embrace caused from the waist down.

"There it is," Darcy whispered in the same impossible tone, holding Ingle's brown eyes in his. The man's entire body thrummed with unexpended energy and he worked up a response, licking his lips several times before did so.

"Master, what can I do for you? You only have to ask."

Ingle had spoken soft so the patron wouldn't hear, but behind them and waiting in the room, the fat man commanded that he hurry. Darcy grinned at Ingle and the man exhaled again, his shoulders dropping and his eyes wet with tears.

"I want to see this face every time I visit," Darcy said and backed away, only dropping contact when at arm's length. Ingle offered an effusive nod, his eyes declaring a dedication that no amount of Oman's abuse could lessen. Darcy turned and entered, closing the door in the keeper's face.

"Enough of that shit! Get over here!" the fat customer barked watching Darcy secure the lock and face him in the dim room. "You will earn your silver tonight, young man, and you will learn to obey," he added, working his belt loose.

Darcy held up one hand, palm out. "You might want to keep those on," he said planning the first move and working out the various scenarios that could follow. A puzzled frown hit the man's round face before he yanked his leather belt free. He flicked it through the air to create a snap and sent Darcy a grin.

"I like that game, too," he said and whipped the thong through the air a second time, not advancing, but he widened his stance.

With a strategy in place, Darcy surged forward and slammed into the patron's flabby embrace. In three well-executed movements, the man was dropped to the floor, face down with one arm securely rammed behind his own back. Darcy shoved a rag deep into his mouth and allowed him to gag and struggle a full minute. Then the man grew tired, stopped resisting and relaxed under Darcy's weight.

It was time to take his blood. Darcy considered his preferred drawing spot, but on a man so large, the neck had zero appeal. There was the crook of the arm... Darcy wrinkled his nose. He didn't want his mouth on the guy at all.

"You would waste all that perfectly good blood, pup?" Elder Pebb asked in his mind, enjoying the show from miles away.

"I think I will, Master," Darcy returned, his lip in a snarl at his victim's aroma. *"He's only one mortal; there are millions more."*

In his mind, his master chuckled and slithered away. Was Pebb impressed or disappointed? Darcy couldn't tell. With one more run at imagining what it might be like to put his lips on the man to draw blood, Darcy made a decision and in one swift move, broke his neck. His Elder transmitted no reaction, so Darcy stood to drag the dead man to the far wall. The brothel keeper would help him dispose of the corpse.

Wait… Ingle is a Cow! Darcy grinned at the thought of the man's blood rushing down his throat.

"So now you would tap Oman's Cow?" Master Pebb sent with humor.

Darcy pictured the tall brown Rakum with the fierce expression. He was there, somewhere in the brothel. He'd had no interactions with the brother, but knew he came from Emil's pack and that was a great honor. He opened the door to the hall and called Ingle's name. In another minute, the man entered, and Darcy closed them in. The expression he'd left Oman's Cow with a half-hour before remained. Ingle *loved* him. *A lot.*

"I need help dumping that guy's body and I need your blood." Darcy looked into his face at the second phrase and Ingle was nodding and already unbuttoning his shirt. Darcy flashed his eyes in appreciation and drew close, his knife making a swift wound. Ingle remained still, arms at his sides, but harder than ever below. Darcy couldn't see the man's thread, he tried. But if he could, he would have toyed with perhaps taking their interaction further.

In his mind, Master Pebb *tsked* at his thought-stream. *"Drink your brother's Cow, fuck your brother's Cow. Ingle's blood-scent has reached Oman's nostrils. You have less than a minute..."*

Still, the master did not sound perturbed and Darcy closed his mouth, healing the wound with the pad of his thumb.

"I will enjoy seeing how you deal with Oman," his master sent at the last and was gone.

To Ingle, he whispered, "Drag him out the back. Your master's headed in and he's not happy about our love affair."

Herr Ingle expressed a few different emotions at his words, but got to work, hefting and yanking the dead man out the back entrance of the room, only looking away from Darcy when time to close the hall door.

Here we go, Darcy said to himself and Master Pebb heard it, too. He ran down scenarios, similarly as he did with the client, but with Oman, the outcomes favored his opponent. The Rakum might attack him without a word—Darcy had broken a well-established tenet about the sanctity of holding Cows. Or his brother might be charmed—their interaction might end with laughter and discussion. And the last possibility, and probably the least likely, he'd use his *ish-mikhan* strengths. Darcy was a new presence among the local packs and only one other Elder besides Pebb knew he was there. In addition, unless someone had a reason to tell him, Oman wouldn't necessarily know Darcy's status. He sent a query to his master but received back the same sentiment as before: "this will be fun to watch."

The door across the room swung wide and Oman stood in the opening, his eyes narrowing as he sought Darcy's gaze.

"Let me get this straight," he said when they locked

eyes. He entered and slammed the door. Two more steps forward, he stopped and crossed thick arms at his chest. "You're all of what? Thirty years old? And you decided I'm lacking as a master to my Cows? Your arrogance is well advanced."

Darcy's mouth formed a half-grin and he thrust his hands in his pockets. Oman had issued questions—he was a talk-first type. Darcy held the man's eye and shrugged his shoulders to his ears.

"I like him," he said with a new grin, "and I thought it might make you come here so I could meet you."

Oman blinked and, in another moment, he uncrossed his arms. "Why did you want to meet me? Aren't you Pebb's little proselyte? The one he's been teaching brothel techniques?"

"I am Master Pebb's ish-mikhan," Darcy said, watching for anything to register in Oman's gaze. This brother was at least a century-and-a-half old and would have learned of the rare brethren skilled in such things.

"No shit?" he said softer and stepped closer. "I never met a fix-it man," he added and again came closer.

Darcy held his eye and when Oman looked away, he scanned Darcy's body. He completed his approach and stood before him, his eyes returning to Darcy's.

"So that's why I'm not mad, eh?" he said very low, his mind apparently tracking over the past minute's conversation. "I looked at your face and wasn't even the least bit upset." He grinned now, his white teeth contrasting against skin as dark as cocoa. "That face… shit." The brother rolled in his bottom lip and held it with his upper teeth. His eyes flit now between Darcy's lips, eyes, and chest. "I'd enjoy that face in my lap."

Darcy widened his eyes. "Did I offend you, Master?"

"Fuck, yeah. You offended me. I'm immensely offended," he said smiling and he lifted his hand to Darcy's smooth cheek.

"Uh-oh," Darcy whispered with false trepidation. *"I messed up."*

"So, fix it, fix-it man," Oman said just as low and licked his lips. "I'm ready. Fix it." And Darcy leaned in.

When Oman left the room, Master Pebb wasn't the only one *very* impressed with Darcy Vandiver.

11

The Bigger Bully

Ellen C. Maze

No matter how mean you are, there's always a bigger bully.

Frankie Varny, Jr. increased his pace; of all days to be running late for band practice. The worst part of it, Frankie was being watched. From his smoking perch across the street, Leroy Tanner's narrow eyes followed him as he jogged down the sidewalk. Frankie knew as well as anyone that nothing good could come from that.

Frankie played bass in a small easy-pop retro band that met above the coffee shop, Tuesdays after dinner. Tonight, directly after dessert, his dad handed him the phone and told him to call his grandmother. A twenty-minute captive conversation later and Frankie would have to really hustle to make it to practice before eight. Now that he'd cut through the alley between Mack's hardware and Janet's Flowers, and the footfalls of the town's meanest bully sounded louder and louder behind him, Frankie regretted leaving the house at all.

"Hey, Nancy, what's the hurry?" a voice barked too close to his ear as a rough hand spun Frankie around. Leroy was not huge, maybe 5'9", but he was wide and mean. He'd flunked out of high school. Even though Frankie was a freshman in college now, his childhood enemy continued to haunt him.

Feigning a semblance of courage, Frankie tried a new tact that he'd been practicing.

"Oh, hey, Leroy. How are ya?"

Leroy didn't seem to have heard him. He shoved him violently with both hands and Frankie stumbled back into the dark shadow of the alley.

"You think you're better than me? Huh? Huh?" The thug didn't want an answer, for as soon as the question left his mouth, he struck Frankie across the jaw with a left hook. Frankie's head snapped back and slammed into the brick wall and his vision blurred.

"Hey, man! No, I don't think—"

Slap! Leroy hit him open-handed with his right palm and then jabbed a body blow into his gut. "Smug bastard! I'll show you who's better and who's a worthless turd!"

Frankie shielded his face with both forearms and withstood multiple blows to his abdomen and a kick to his groin that dropped him to his knees. Through a moving red haze, the shape of his enemy filled his vision. A fist in his hair forced his face into the ground and he soon felt Leroy shuffling through his back pocket for the wallet mom gave him for his 19th birthday two nights ago. Let him have it; Frankie could get another one.

Frankie breathed through his mouth as Leroy shouted curses down on him. When the bully's camouflage work boot came down on his head, Frankie whimpered and the lights went out.

Leroy left the alley, fanning out the ten-dollar bills. Seventy bucks meant a fairly comfortable beer binge with Jake and Gary. Leroy walked faster, shoved the money into his front jeans pocket, and wiped the nerd's blood from his knuckles to his shirt. Like a war wound, the blood would show the stupid cows passing him tonight on the street that he was dangerous. Leroy growled and faked a lunge at a man and his wife who stared at him too long as he passed. *Jerks, all of 'em,* he thought as he fell into a trot.

Gary's garage was only a block away and the boys could hit the town as soon as he arrived. Only Jake had a running vehicle, and Leroy vowed under his breath that if he got to Gary's before their driver he'd mess him up plenty. Nobody was going to screw up the evening Leroy had planned for them. After a few rounds of beer and pool at Kippy's Bar & Billiards, they'd walk the bartender, Polly, to her car. The woman got off at eleven and she had it coming. Last week, when Leroy and the boys followed her into the parking lot after work, they'd scared her pretty good before Kippy came out and ruined the party. Tonight, Leroy and Gary would grab her, throw her into Jake's car and take her back to the garage. Private parties were best, after all.

Leroy slowed to a fast walk as he reached 5th Avenue. He wasn't even breathing hard; it paid to hit the gym in the mornings. His sad-ass mother paid for the membership in an effort to connect with him, but she could go to hell. He'd take her money, but he'd never return her affection. She just didn't deserve it; ran off his father when he was only five and never stopped trying to make it up to him.

Leroy cursed his mother aloud and then stopped

dead. A shadow had passed his position and disappeared again to his right. It was large, upright, and moved like a man. Who in their right mind would stalk Leroy Tanner? He was the king of the night here in Jackson Heights. Leroy looked both ways and then up to the fire escapes of the flanking buildings. If anyone was there, he was mighty stealthy. Just to cover his bases, Leroy called out a taunt followed by a stream of expletives and threats. When no one answered and the alley remained still, Leroy sighed angrily and resumed his pace toward the light at the end of the dim alley. Sounds of laughter wafted from Gary's straight ahead and he grinned until the shadow crossed his path and disappeared once more. Leroy whirled around, brandishing his hastily-opened switch blade at the same time.

"I'm sick a playin' with you, jerkwad!" he hissed, his eyes darting back and forth. Twenty feet behind him, his pals whistled at something and laughed. Leroy thought about calling for them. He considered turning and running out of the alley as fast as he could. But he did neither. He repeated his previous statement and spat into the darkness.

Ooph!

Without warning, a fist knocked out his breath and Leroy stared into the hard gaze of his attacker. Hooded, Caucasian, and very angry, the killer removed his fist and thrust it again, deeper this time, his opposite arm holding Leroy in place. Leroy spat blood onto his enemy's face and noticed, for the first time, a searing pain in his gut. He'd been stabbed, and by a much bigger knife than his own.

Almond tightened his grip on the hunting knife and rotated his wrist forcefully both ways until his surprised victim mumbled twice and gave up the ghost. It was a good kill, a clean kill. Wiping the eight-inch serrated blade on his pants, Almond let the guy drop to the littered cement and backed into the shadows. The guy might not be discovered until morning, but there was no way of knowing for sure. Almond hugged the brick wall with his back and made his way back to the main road in shadows. When he reached the end of the building, he shrugged off his hood with a swift movement of his shoulders, and fell into the flow of jolly pedestrians.

The night was a comfortable 68 degrees and a dozen locals walked arm-in-arm or side-by-side all around him. Theaters, clubs, bars, and restaurants lined the street on both sides, and Almond walked nonchalantly to avoid drawing attention. He blended in, a rugged build—not fat, not skinny, a common face—not handsome, not ugly, and tired clothing—faded navy-blue hoodie over shredded black jeans and dusty black boots. He never turned heads, which worked out fine since his dream was to be invisible. He had a mission and drawing attention to himself only interfered, never helped.

The thick thug in the alley was part of his mission. The beady eyes, swaggering manner, and buzzed-off dirty blond hair made the moron in the alley the perfect target. Every time Almond ended one of those types, his soul was soothed a little bit more than before. Each time he watched the life drain from those soulless eyes, Oppy was once again laid to rest.

His mother's father, Oppy took seven-year-old Almond in when his parents were killed in a plane crash. Almond's childhood ended the first weekend after a jaunt to Oppy's secluded lake cabin. When Almond was old enough, he fought back. When he was strong enough, he stabbed his grandfather in the gut with the guy's own hunting knife. Now, twenty years later, killing Oppys was the only thing that gave Almond pleasure.

Almond reached his Geo Metro and fell into the cracked vinyl seat-cover. It wasn't long before he passed the "Come back soon!" sign as you head out of town. After two miles of open farmland, the dark sky blanketed thick forests that bled into the Tuskegee National Forest. Almond considered his condition, but all he felt was bliss. Utter joy at ridding his universe of another disgusting Oppy clone. A smile touched the edges of his mouth and he relaxed into the stiff chair just as flashing blue lights up ahead snagged his attention. *The police!*

Thinking fast, Almond sat erect, fastened his belt, and slowed the vehicle. It would be virtually impossible for the cops to know he'd just dispatched the jerk back in town. A bit closer and he noted the shield on the closest patrol car: sheriff's department. This was some local crap, not a concern of his. Almond came to a stop at the makeshift roadblock and rolled down his window. A snappily-uniformed deputy met his car and leaned casually in to speak.

"Sir, we're stopping everyone heading into the Forest," the deputy said, one hand now pointing into the dark trees. "A farmer was mauled to death tonight and we don't know yet what kind of animal we're dealing with. Could be a bear or a rabid wolf. You headin' home?"

Almond nodded and purposefully loosened his grip on the steering wheel to appear calm. "Yessir. I live on Birdie Lane, just before you enter the Forest."

"Uh-huh, okay. Go straight home, get inside, and lock your door, okay? In the morning, we'll come by and check on you and your neighbors."

"Yessir," Almond said as the cop stood off his car and took a step back. "Thanks. I'll be careful."

The cop waved him through and Almond minded the rules the rest of the way home. When he reached his cabin, he left the car and stretched toward the full moon. He loved to look for Oppys on a full moon—he always seemed to have the best luck then.

A howl split the silence and for an instant, Almond's breath hitched. He recovered almost immediately and completed his stretch. Taking a step toward his unlit porch, the howl sounded again, much closer. Almond pulled his knife from the sheath in his lower back and faced the woods. He feared neither man nor beast, and tonight, he felt strong enough to overcome anyone who dared oppose him. A rustle to his right egged him on and he stepped toward the tree-line. Before he took three steps, a large black shape leapt from the bushes and slammed into him full force. Almond fell hard onto his rear, flipped himself over in an instant, and prepared to stand. Before he could bring his knees under him, a weight, heavy and moving, landed on his middle, forcing him to abandon the thought of rising, and instead, pushed his lower half into the moist leaves.

"Get off me!" Almond shouted, but the thing continued its attack unimpeded.

Fire erupted across his shoulders as knife-like claws scraped repeatedly across his back and a wicked growl filled the clearing. Almond's hoodie and T-shirt were shredded within seconds and his bare back couldn't withstand the attack. With deep lacerations profusely leaking blood, Almond collapsed to the wet earth, his mouth filling with mud. Roaring now more like a lion, his attacker increased its efforts to skin him alive and Almond lost consciousness.

An explosion from the not-too-distant north distracted Kuma from his fugue. The crimson-haze that filled his mind as well as his soul filtered slowly away as he became aware of the possible danger approaching from behind. Leaping off the dead human, Kuma took cover in the tall, unkempt bushes that lined the cabin's clearing. He couldn't recall how he knew to avoid the ones with the loud stick, but he knew with every fiber of his being that he should run. The ones that carried the stick carried lights in their hands and wore a curious star on their chests. Kuma hunkered down as low as possible and watched the stick-men arrive.

The first to pass his position seemed familiar. His scent, his shape, even the sound of his voice triggered memories from deep within, but Kuma could form no coherent thought regarding the sensation. It was almost as if he *should* know him and know how to react, but Kuma saw only red and desired only to open the human up with sharp claws.

"Over here!" the stick-man said, and Kuma marveled at the words. He understood them, and morbid fear possessed him at the same time. More rustling brought more stick-men to his proximity and Kuma considered bursting out. Before he could make up his mind, the one he recognized pushed into his cover and called out loudly for his fellows.

"I see him!" he yelled, his loud stick coming up to Kuma's eye level. Kuma roared at the top of his voice and leapt straight for the human blocking his escape. With a deafening sound, the stick erupted fire.

"I got him! By God, I got him!" Frankie Sr. shouted as his fellow deputies reached his twenty. For a week, local farmers had been reporting missing sheep, and most recently, mauled livestock. Tonight, Farmer Mason was found mutilated outside his barn two miles away. Frankie Sr. cocked his rifle and fired one more round into the animal's chest. It was down, and as he half-expected, it didn't look quite animal enough for his taste.

Without sharing his theories with his fellow officers, Frankie Sr. had been suspecting a supernatural perp from the start. As soon as he noted the strange man-wolf footprints left at all of the mauling scenes, Frankie Sr. figured whatever was doing the killing was neither man nor beast, but something in between. Tonight, just in case he was right, he'd loaded his Remington with silver bullets. They seemed to have done the trick. Before his eyes, the wolf-shaped man began to shrink, shrivel, and mutate back into the man he'd been before his transformation. By the time his pals shined their beams on the bloody mess, they recognized the Mason kid. He'd been a sweet guy, a little slow in the head, but friendly and generally helpful around the farm.

"Joshua Mason?" the deputy on his right asked the air. "That kid's been doin' all this killin'? That don't make sense."

"That weren't no Joshua Mason made them slashes in Farmer Mason's back, I tell ya." The other deputy offered and spat a wad of tobacco.

Frankie Sr. didn't add his two cents. He was city enough to know when to keep his mouth shut and country enough to believe in monsters. Joshua Mason had somehow gotten himself mixed up with a werewolf. Now…how to find the one that made him…

Buzzzz!

Frankie Sr. whipped his walkie from its holder and pressed the button. "You got Varny, go ahead."

"Varny, Doc Miller called. Your son was beaten unconscious tonight. Some kids found him in an alley. He's okay, but you might want to go by the hospital and see him."

Frankie Sr. calmed the nervous knot in his belly and told the dispatcher he would. Leaving the body of Joshua Mason to his coworkers, he headed for his patrol car.

"Damn bullies," he mumbled, "the world would be such a nice place if everyone would just be NICE."

In his car, he phoned ahead to alert his wife of their son's condition. Wouldn't do to have her find out from a neighbor. Small towns, small minds, and all that. Frankie Sr. zoomed back into town and ran his lights for good measure. Tomorrow morning, he'd arrest that no good Tanner, who'd been picking on his boy for the better part of ten years. Tomorrow night—he'd hunt down the other werewolf. The town couldn't support more than one and Frankie Sr. had been there the longest.

It was going to be a busy day.

12

The Bruise

Ellen C. Maze

A bruise can change everything. Just ask Patty.

The bruise came up on a Friday. Patty hadn't noticed it when she dressed; who looks back there anyway? Yet, she should have checked, because Jonesy saw it. He stood behind her every weekday in third-period Chorale, raised above her row six inches by the platformed step. He's the one that always noticed her shortcomings and shared them with the class. A smidge of dandruff today, Fatty-Patty? I'll tell the tenor section. Tag hanging out of your dress? I'll tell those bass guys. Did you just fart? I'm sure it was you. I'll tell the baritones. Oh, what's that spot? I think you started your period, Fat-Pat. Better go to the office, and while you're gone, I'll tell the altos.

Today, he tapped the back of her bare shoulder and she winced. "Your daddy beating on you again, Pat-Rat?" he said, looking her right in the face. Jonesy was tall, tanned, and cute; the rodent-like glitter in his green eyes is all that revealed his evil inclination to gossip and slander the (slightly) overweight masses.

Patty didn't answer and whirled her eyes front. She lifted a hand to her right shoulder and touched where he had indicated.

Wince.

Something was definitely wrong. Patty asked the girl in front of her on the lower step to move aside. The girl next to her also moved as if she needed more room—which she *didn't.* Jonesy called her fat, but she was only a little pudgy. *Maybe* she weighed twenty pounds more than Melissa Harper, and maybe thirty pounds more than Danielle Freed, but hey—she didn't have roll upon roll upon roll of jiggling lard flapping all around when she walked. Shit. I mean, *dang...*

Chillaxed to the max as always, Ms. Poppa dismissed her to the ladies' by mere eye contact. The class was an easy A and no one stood out as a truly promising talent. Patty walked briskly out the door and into the wide, clean hallway. Daddy (who never, ever hit her, ever) paid for the private school she attended and when he visited monthly she thanked him every time. A girl's education was important. To Patty, it meant going to college for her MRS degree. Make good grades, get into a good college, find a good husband. See? *MRS. Degree* ...Clever.

Patty's identical twin sister, Latty (short for Laticia), lived with Dad and attended public school. From their frequent emails and texts, Latty shared that although she would prefer private school she had "so many friends here. I don't want to leave them." Patty, on the other hand, only had one friend—Latty. So why didn't she go live with Dad, too? Maybe it was because he—

"Hey, *Petty,*" lean mean Melissa Harper said exiting the bathroom. Patty said nothing and squeezed in, the thinner girl purposefully blocking the door a few seconds too long. "See ya in gym class, Petty."

Patty waited for the door to close and she turned her back to the large framed floor-length mirror on the far wall. She had worn the school's approved tank-shirt option because the summer would never end. The heat was the main reason Dad moved to North Alabama. Might not sound like a big difference, but anyone who lived in Montgomery, Alabama, knew that anywhere north of Birmingham was significantly cooler in the dogdays of summer. Plus, Patty had always been a healthy perspirer.

"Eww!" she hissed when her wound came into view. Patty stepped rearward and examined the bruise more closely. It was utterly disgusting. Colored various shades of gray and purple, spanning five inches across in a circular shape, the wound featured two puckering wounds two inches apart and dead center. The edges of these punctures remained red and painful to the touch. They must have bled at some point, Patty surmised. Had she somehow missed a pillow doused in red this morning? No, definitely not. She had made the bed before she ate breakfast to avoid hearing her mom's nagging. Patty touched it a few more times, grimaced, and headed for the nurse's station. If she played her cards right she would be sent home. Even if they kept her at school, at least she'd miss the rest of Chorale and part of 4th. Patty put on her sad eyes and pushed open the nurse's door.

Patty hadn't shown the bruise to her mom so Saturday morning she wore a T-shirt that covered it. All weekend she avoided stressing her back or shoulders and watched for signs of healing. Sunday night before she went to sleep, she checked it in her bathroom mirror. It was no longer purple—the expanse had shrunk to maybe three inches across and was shaded in light grays. The punctures had scabbed sufficiently that they looked like they would close without infection. Patty nodded to the air and headed to bed.

Monday morning at six a.m. Latty texted her.

"Guuy ko d*u," it read. Patty waited for a correction as she dressed for the morning. Before she shrugged on her dark blue uniform polo, she turned her back to the mirror. "What?!" she yelped. The wound was back and worse than before. Mom trotted into the room and called her name. Patty stuck her head out of her bathroom door. "Sorry, Mom. Stubbed my toe. I'm almost ready."

Mom's face relaxed and she blew Patty a kiss. Patty locked the bathroom door and backed to the mirror. How did it come back? After looking all around the small room for any signs of blood or a place to be punctured, she shrugged on her shirt and crossed to her bed. No blood, nothing sharp, no reason at all for a young woman of eighteen to have stab wounds in her back Monday morning. Okay, they were punctures, really. Two, in the exact same location as before. In fact, it was the same wound, only reopened and re-injured.

Patty's cell rang Latty's assigned tone and she answered it. "Your text is—"

"Klllo ppoo tuu faahhh dshhh d-shhh."

"Latty," Patty said and listened. The voice didn't sound precisely like Latty, but it was close. And of course, Latty spoke English, not whatever this was.

"Haaaa juuck ck ck."

"Latty?" Patty said wondering if she should be alarmed. The voice that might have been her twin didn't sound stressed. If anything, it sounded sort of like someone on drugs or talking in their sleep.

Click.

The call disconnected and Patty dialed her sister walking to the stairs. No answer. It went to voicemail and she left Latty a message. At the table, Mom gestured for her to sit down.

"I have some news about your sister," she said and waited for Patty to sit. Mom didn't look upset so Patty relaxed. "Latty's coming to live with us again. Your dad and his wife are moving to Europe to be near her folks."

Patty folded her arms on the tabletop. "When?" She loved Latty, they had fun together, but when her sister decided to move in with Dad, she had been adamant it was the only thing that would make her happy. Could Patty make her happy enough to not regret coming back?

"Tonight," Mom said and reached over to rub Patty's arm.

"Can I stay home from school and get her room ready?" Patty asked, certain her mom would refuse.

"Sure, honey," she said and stood. "I have a few patients to see and I should be done around three. Dad's dropping her off at five."

Patty gave Mom a hug and watched her grab her nurse's bag and leave. Patty waited the appropriate interval to allow her mother to drive away and she opened the fridge. One more Poptart and one more bowl of cereal and she'd go remove her storage boxes from Latty's room.

Ting!

Latty's text tone sounded and Patty looked at the screen.

"Kllloo pourrrrth */ th th= darl ck ck."

Patty copied the letters and symbols and pasted them into a new text message. She hit send and finished her Froot Loops.

By five o'clock, Latty's room was ready. Patty had heated up some leftovers that Mom set out and a *C.S.I. Miami* marathon played on the huge flat screen TV in the den. Patty lounged on the leather sectional, feet propped up before her so she could frame Horatio's face with her two feet any time the camera came in for a close-up. *Sunglasses go on—foot frame!* It was a fun time. Horatio Caine cared about victims. *Foot frame!* Patty giggled.

Mom walked behind the sofa and leaned in for a smooch. Her hand landed on Patty's covered bruise and she shrieked. Mom jumped back and put both hands to her mouth. "What?"

"Nothing," Patty covered quickly. "Scared me."

Mom fanned her face with one hand and grinned. "Scared me worse!"

Patty forced a laugh and they both heard the front door open in the other side of the house.

"Patty!" her sister called and trotted into the den.

"Latty!" Patty responded and heaved from her reclining position to hug her twin. The sisters were indeed identical in DNA, but not in body type. Somewhere during puberty, Patty grew heavy while Latty grew thin. Now they looked like a before and after pic, but Patty put that out of her mind. Dad's new wife was the only one uncouth enough to mention the disparity and she was about to be far away in Europe. *HashtagLOL. HashtagSadNotSad.*

"I missed you!" her sister said and hugged her tight. Dad hadn't come in so Patty waited while Latty embraced Mom and then followed her upstairs. In Latty's room, her sister dropped her bag onto her bed and massaged her tired neck muscles. "That's too heavy. I brought you a present."

Patty stepped up and watched her sister pull a large hardbound book from her luggage. *Insomnia* by Stephen King. Her copy had been lost at school when they were twelve.

"Aw, thanks!" Patty received it and flipped it open. It was signed by the author. "Get out!"

Latty nodded. "Yep. Daddy took me to see him at Barnes and Noble in Atlanta. I knew you'd like it."

Patty held the book in her left hand and hugged Latty with her right. Her sister grunted when they released.

"What's wrong?"

"Nothing," she said and started unloading her folded clothing. Patty helped her and by the time the clock struck six, they hopped down to watch another episode of Horatio and the Most Gorgeous People of Miami.

At midnight, Patty and Latty went upstairs to talk. Mom said since Patty's grades were good, she could be sick one more day to catch up with Latty. The two planned to giggle their way back to the present. Patty wanted to talk about boys, and thankfully, Latty had the best stories.

"I had three boyfriends last year," Latty shared, her

blue eyes sparkling. In delightful detail, she described petting sessions Patty only read about in novels. When she reached the part where Phil Milton nearly got to third base, Patty's cell chimed.

Ting!

Latty's assigned tone.

Patty puzzled at her sister and grabbed her cell beside her.

"llooooo &FD$ ook ck ck ck.!"

Patty giggled and showed the screen to Latty. "Your phone is sending me some crazy texts."

She didn't expect Latty to yank her cell away and run into the bathroom. Latty slammed and locked the door and Patty rolled onto her back, wondering what the hell just happened. After a few seconds, she called from the bed, "Latty? You okay?"

"Asshole!" she heard on the other side.

"Um, what? Me?" Patty asked. Latty opened the door.

"No, George." She handed the cell to Patty and tromped back to the bed. She'd left it open for Patty to read the screen. Under the latest garble-de-gook text, Latty had responded, "ASS!"

And then on the grey side, it read Patty's address. "What?" She walked to the bed and showed the phone to her sister. "Who has your phone?"

"I don't want to talk about it," she said and rolled onto her stomach cross-wise on the full bed.

"Whoever it is knows where I live?"

Latty rolled her head to see Patty's face. "Where *I* live, thank you."

Patty looked at the closed bedroom door, still trying to sort it out. "But you didn't type that—it did. He did. Is it a he? Who has your phone?"

"I told you. George."

"How long has George had it? I've gotten a couple of calls, too. I thought it was you."

Latty rolled over to sit up. "What? He called you? What did he say?"

Patty pointed at the text. "This, only in a voice that sounded sort of like you sleeping."

Latty scratched her head. "No, it was him. He has a high voice." She sighed and slapped her leg. "Asshole. He shouldn't be texting you."

Patty wanted to be nice, but there was still the issue of George knowing her address. "He typed this in—why? Is he coming here?"

Now Latty looked unsure. "Yeah... wait..." She rose to her feet and took the phone back. After deftly flying her pretty fingers across the keyboard, she hit send and waited.

"What are you doing?"

"I'm gonna find out how he had your address. I was so mad he took my phone that I didn't notice that."

"When did he get it?"

Latty shrugged her shoulders and frowned.

"Did you hurt yourself?" Patty went to her side and tried to see down the back of her big yellow T-shirt. Latty moved away and the phone chimed its *ting!* again. Latty read the screen and looked at Patty.

"You seeing George behind my back?" Her lips were drawn tight and her eyes squeezed small; she really believed Patty was chatting up her man.

Patty laughed and shook her head. "No. What is he saying?"

Latty held out the screen. On the blue side, Latty had typed, "Hw'd U get this adrss?"

"PATTY," the screen read on the grey side.

Patty shook her head and stared at the readout. Latty walked to the window and peeked between the mini-blinds into the night.

Ting!

Patty looked at the screen as it refreshed in her hand. George had texted, PATTY again followed by the thumbs-up emoji. Latty jogged to her side and yanked the phone away again. She typed furiously and watched for a response. Nothing happened. After waiting two minutes, Patty gave up and sat on the edge of the bed. Latty waited another fifteen minutes and then set the cell on the bedcovers between them. They lay back and went back to discussing boys and Latty finally decided to talk about George.

"He's kinda special," she said and rubbed her neck. "Maybe he looked us up by Facebook or SnapChat and got the address that way. He's got computer skills, just not very many people skills."

"Or language skills," Patty said and Latty laughed.

"Yeah."

"What do you think the phone calls were about? The weird breathing and weird language?"

Latty shook her head in the low light. "I never heard him on the phone before. He speaks English, it's just all broken up."

"Ya'll make out?" Patty asked. So far, all the boys she mentioned had been awesome kissers. This one, no mention of that at all.

"Yeah," Latty said and fell quiet. She switched off the lamp on her side of the bed and the room fell dark. "Good night, Patty. I'm glad I'm home."

"Me, too," Patty said and stared at the ceiling fan in the dark. Their bedrooms shared a bathroom between them and the nightlight by the toilet provided a somber blue light.

Before long, Latty was snoring softly like a puppy and Patty rolled to her right side facing away from her twin. A hallucination crouched before the bathroom door and she looked it over. It could have been a lump of laundry four feet high. Had she left a chair there? Patty closed her eyes languidly and reopened them. The shape was closer. It still was featureless with the nightlight behind it. Once more, Patty slow-blinked and this time, it had reached her bed. Patty inhaled to scream, but the shape covered her mouth and eased her off the covers.

"Shhhhhh," the shape said in her ear and dragged her upward into its arms as if she weighed nothing. Her back pressed against the shape's front and to her numbing flesh, it felt human, torso, arms, legs, neck and head... Patty did not kick or struggle, every muscle in her body fast asleep. All except, that is, her eyes and ears. The shape pressed its warm mouth to her cheek and she felt its lips on her ear. *"Patty-Patty. My-my-Patty,"* it sang, breathy and high, like an adolescent boy.

Patty wanted to speak, shout, or even sing along, but her tongue remained as paralyzed as the rest of her body. Cool fingers tugged on the back of her T-shirt collar, first gently and with care, but then with a jerk that ripped the fabric. Pressed up against its form, Patty's wound was now exposed to the shape's face. The shape pressed something wet and hot to her bruise and she recognized the sensation of long teeth penetrating her flesh. In her mind, she pictured a venomous snake's fangs punching into an orange. Then there was the suction. Patty's eyes grew wider and she tried again to move. No go. Wet slurpy noises filled her ears and she closed her eyes to desperate tears.

"My-my-Patty, Patty-Patty, Love-love-love-my-Patty," it sang, this time in her mind, deep behind her inner ear. Patty thought to shake her head, but instead, she blacked out.

The six a.m. bladder alarm woke Patty from a dream about snakes and wolves and helpless campers. She shuffled to the bathroom, peed with the door open, and then walked back to bed where her sister slept facing her, still snoring little puppy puffs. Patty yanked the covers down—apparently she'd gone to sleep on top of them last night—and when she did, her shoulder ached worse than before. Putting her fingers to her back, she realized her shirt was ripped at the collar. She touched the bruise and found the punctures raised and tacky. Latty rolled over just then and her giant sleeping shirt didn't go with her. Across the back of her shoulder, closer to her neck than Patty's, her twin had a matching bruise. Patty knelt on the bed and leaned toward her, examining it in the bright morning light. Similar shape, similar size, same color. Slightly different location, but still same vicinity. Only difference? Patty's was fresh. Latty's looked several days old.

Patty carefully relaxed onto her back and stared at the white sunlight on the ceiling. The dull ache in her wound prevented her from falling back to sleep so she pondered the smallish form that must have been George. What *was* he? (besides a monster, of course). Why was he so small? He had held Patty up to his mouth, but her paralyzed knees had been bent. That meant he was what, five feet? And had he a face? Patty only recalled a shape. Yet he had teeth—long fangs.

Ting!

Patty reached for the phone, but Latty had secretly awakened and she yanked it up first. Patty read the screen while in her sister's hand.

"lvvvvv Ptty &2 ck ck ck lvvvvv Ltty."

Latty looked at Patty without turning her head, her eyes small and angry. She typed a reply and didn't hide it from her twin.

"We lv U2"

Latty handed Patty the phone and rolled away, sighing.

Patty stared at the phone. George was typing something so she watched and waited.

"He'll come every three days," Latty said in a sad voice. "He doesn't always need blood. Sometimes he'll just hold me. I think he's cold."

Patty remained quiet and watched the screen.

"We'll share him. I don't mind." Latty took a deep breath and sighed again. "I guess he likes big girls, too."

Patty jerked her head toward Latty. Never, never, never, never (*hashtagTimesInfinity*) had her sister ever called her fat. Dad had. Mina (wife number two) had. But never Latty. Patty's eyes filled with water.

Because the app was open, the cell made a nearly inaudible *whir* when George replied. Patty read the screen through a veil of salty tears.

"Grg lvPtty Mort thn Ltty."

Patty sniffled and sat up. She rolled out of bed and took the phone into the bathroom. "Really?" she texted and locked both doors.

"MorMorMormormormormormormormor," he texted back. Then another *whir* as seven heart-eyes emoji filled her screen.

Patty took a screenshot and emailed it to herself. Then she pressed his love-declaration message until the delete option appeared. Once the message disappeared, she went to her photos and deleted the screenshot. Latty didn't need to know she was too skinny for George. Patty smiled and got in the shower. Now she had a boyfriend, too.

13

Lilith

Taylor Vogt

The world has been created in six days, as in the Book of Genesis. Lilith, the first woman, has been relegated to the Earth after being kicked out of the Garden of Eden. Samael the Archangel of Death approaches her to become the first demon, the Queen of Hell, and shepherd humanity as it evolves on the new planet.

The world was new. The first dew to ever drip off the luscious broad-leafed forests onto nubile soil below breathed life into what would come be known as the Earth. Mighty rivers the planet over began flowing as the tectonic plates far below the surface yawned into existence, shuddered out of their eternal slumber as the Lord willed them to begin clashing. This Earth had been incubating for far too long, though it had just been six nights in the realm of the divine, and now Man and animal alike inherited the grounds where giant creatures had roamed eons before. The apple had been bitten, and with it, the intelligent Man had descended onto its shores. Someday the intelligent Man would corral its less evolved counterparts, but at this moment the wilds were untamed and flourishing.

On the edge of a cliff overseeing a great deciduous forest, a woman in rags sat with her long legs dangling. She swung them back and forth, hands planted on the red, fractured rock, and even though she was looking out at the expanse it seemed as though she was lost somewhere else. Her long black hair got picked up in the wind, tossing it around like the tumultuous thoughts in her head.

"It's all yours. That is an indisputable fact," a man voice said behind her, making the woman turn her head to look back. He stood with a black robe on, his hair even darker than hers, with heavy bags burned into the skin under his eyes that almost looked like makeup.

"You should leave me be, Samael," the woman said, turning back to look out over paradise. She gripped down on fistfuls of dirt as the man sat down next to her.

"Lilith," he said, positioning himself so his legs were dangling as well. "You should be thankful."

The woman scoffed, turning her head away from him. "Why? Because the Lord determined I should live in exile instead of being relegated to oblivion?" she asked, biting anger to her tone.

"You think God is that petty? He didn't believe your case was wrong," Samael said, without turning to look over at her. He was awed by the beauty of the world he was seeing for the first time. He had yet to lay a foot upon this world before he had come to talk to her.

Lilith bit her plump lip and bore the pressure of her fist down harder on the granules of red sand she was holding. "Then why did he kick me out of Eden?" she asked.

"He didn't. You left. Your leaving Eden confirmed his test of you," Samael said.

Lilith whipped her head back around and burnt her eyes into Samael's, who had turned to face her. "What the hell are you talking about?" Lilith shouted before she relented and threw the dirt in her right fist out in the void between them and the rest of the forest. "Metatron told me! He told me that I wasn't fit to be in Eden! They kicked me out!"

"Lilith," Samael said calmly, making her turn back to him with a look of disrepair and longing. She was hurt. "When God decided to create humans, he knew that Men were selfish and destructive, power-hungry, and unfaithful. He wanted to test the first Man, Adam, and he created you to see how things would play out. When you voiced your concerns about equality, he wasn't punishing you when he sent you to oblivion. You had certainly passed the test, so to speak. He needed to learn more about Man, so he kept you safe until you could truly live out your purpose," Samael said, continuing his calmed tone.

Lilith didn't say anything for a moment but drew in an audibly deep breath before bringing her clasped hands up to her face. She clenched her eyes and exhaled. "I would take issue with that if I didn't know that angels cannot lie to a human," she said.

"I am not lying, but in that same vein, you are no longer human," Samael said.

Lilith opened her eyes and peered out of the corner of them at Samael, who offered her a small smile. "Explain your words, angel," Lilith said, lowering her hands.

"Hell is real now," Samael said.

A look of shock overtook Lilith's face, as she slowly lowered her hands to her lap. "So it's come to that, has it? Adam screwed things over that badly?" she asked.

Samael nodded a little bit, before turning to look out over the forest. "Eve convinced him to take a bit of the forbidden fruit," Samael said.

"The fool," Lilith whispered, hushed by the stark realization of what her former lover had done. "That's what happens when you make a woman who borrows her life essence from the original soul of a man," she said, solemn sadness dripping on her words.

"And that is exactly why you are here. Adam and Eve are out there, somewhere, and they are going to make the line of Seth. Cain and Abel will have their problems, but the line of Seth will create the lineage of Intelligent Man. And if you choose to accept it, you will use your original female human soul to spark intelligence in the offspring of the lower man," Samael said. He turned to Lilith and held his hand out to her. "Take my hand and become the first demon. Take my hand and choose from mankind who you will impart your gift of a perfect original soul onto. Take my hand, and become my partner overseeing the punishment of men in this new hell that has been created," Samael said.

"You," Lilith began, catching herself. "You didn't appeal to the Lord himself for my salvation did you?" she asked, an air of unbelieving her line of questioning overshadowed by a firm belief she already knew what he was going to say.

Samael nodded slowly. "I did. I thought you would be the perfect partner to see this wild experiment through beside." Samael smiled a bit. "You are the only immortal I ever truly enjoyed standing beside to converse, and I think you're the perfect being to walk this new charge beside," he said.

Lilith looked down at her hand, marred red by the soil she had been clutching, before looking back over at Samael. Slowly she raised her hand, but gained confidence in her decision and reached out to grasp his hand.

The moment their hands touched, fabric colored purple, black, and gold began materializing on her arm and spread out over her body. As the last of the fabric materialized around her feet in the form of black shoes, two horns began protruding out of her head. It wasn't painful, and when it was done they were long with an accentuated spiral, black and golden rings adorning them like they were painted on. She looked regal, like a queen. She peered behind her to see a long, thick black tail with the shape of a heart formed by the flesh at the end of it. Though she couldn't see it, her eyes had changed to become a light green with purple irises.

"I'm scared of this new power I feel, Samael," Lilith said. "It feels different, and I cannot tell whether that is a good thing or something I should run from."

"Then you are just like every creature on this planet right now. None of us truly know what will come of this new dawning age. The only thing we know is that we all have a part to play, and we must play it," Samael said.

Lilith licked her lips, as they changed to a light blue while her skin continued to change its pigment to a darker shade of purple. She flapped the large bat-like wings on her back once. "Then I will play my part. And I will do it alongside you, as my partner," Lilith said. She gripped down on Samael's hand a bit, and he returned the gesture.

The two of them turned to the expanse of the forest before them, taking in the new world that had just been given agency to determine its own future.

14

The Princess and the King

Kay Fondren

Once upon a time there was a prince who was forced to venture out in search of a princess to marry. His father the King had given him strict rules to follow, the most important being, the lady he chose must be a real princess.

Young Prince Gaither travelled throughout his own kingdom and then rode his trusty steed across the world in his quest. He traveled far and near meeting ladies who swore they were indeed princesses, only to find they had lied. Most were more than willing to do anything he chose to prove their worth and merit. Young Gaither sowed his wild oats with hundreds of wanton women and learned not only about the wiles of the world, but the ways he could please his princess once he found her.

Gwenevive of Rochester was one of his first conquests; or was he hers, as the story would tell. Beautiful Gwenevive lured him to her home made of stone and mud, promising him she had a daughter who would be the princess he had long been searching for. Once inside, he sat on a woven chair of thatch and vine and waited for her to appear.

"My lady," he called out when Gwenevive had left the room. "You must hurry for I have other places to go in search of my bride."

Gwenevive came out wearing only her silken robe exposing her shoulders and a hint of her breast. "Come with me," she whispered as Gaither stood. "I will show you your princess." Gaither followed her down the dark corridor and into a faintly lit room adorned with silk tapestry and a carpeted floor fit for a King.

"Lay here," she said as she motioned toward the huge bed with the plush headboard and silky coverings. "Rest your eyes and you will soon see something unlike anything you have ever seen before."

Gaither leaned back and soon was staring at the candlelit chandelier gently swaying above the bed.

"It's hypnotic, isn't it?" she asked. "It can take you to places you never thought existed."

Gwenevive slipped from her robe and lay next to him gazing into the chandelier's light. Her hand slid gently against his tightly fitted riding slacks and then beneath them as she stroked his young and now throbbing erection.

"You love this, don't you?" she whispered as her warm breath tickled his ear. "Let me show you something," she said as her fingers unlaced the ties and freed his manhood. "You'll never forget me, I promise."

Gwenevive watched as Prince Gaither closed his eyes and allowed her to touch him. Her strokes were gentle as he felt himself pulsing and coming more to life than he'd ever been. He wanted more of this woman. Her daughter the princess wasn't even a passing thought as his penis throbbed and surrendered to her taunting fingertips.

Gwenevive rolled onto him feeling him glide easily into her body as she teased him with her flexing muscles and light thrusts.

"AUGHH," he moaned as he felt himself growing tense and his blood coursed through his loins, demanding he take over and end this punishment of making him wait. Gaither rolled over and began pushing himself deeper and deeper as she gushed and screamed with delight. Soon he was one with her in his lust as he relieved his tension and fell across her body unable to gather his thoughts.

"May the Gods have mercy on us," he said as he realized what he'd done with this woman. Breathlessly he exclaimed, "Madame, I feel you have lied to me and there was never a princess or even a daughter living here! Why would you lure me into your bed chamber in such a manner?"

"Because I've been with many men but never a real prince, and now I can say I have." She put her silken robe back on as she looked at his still trembling body and smiled. "You did your job and you did it well, now be off with you. I hope you find your princess but if you cannot, remember I am here and will wait for your return for there are many lessons still to be taught."

Gaither quickly ran to his steed and like the wind they were soon out of sight. He was weary and disappointed after even more months of searching to no avail.

How can I ever go home again, he thought, *I have found no princess and until I do, so the king says, I cannot return.*

Gaither rode his steed back to the palace and begged his father to allow him to come home.

"You dare come back here without a bride?" the King said angrily, "and you want to remain here as my son?"

"Yes, Father," Gaither most humbly replied. "I have ridden my horse throughout the world. I have been used, abused, lied to, and even taken advantage of. Father, there are women who take men as a man would a woman and use them for their own pleasure and gratification. It was a horrible experience."

The King stared at his son in disbelief because even a male commoner would gladly allow a woman to invite them into their bed chamber and use them until there was nothing left to use.

"If this has taught me anything, it's this," the King said. "You are a fool and unworthy of a real princess, for you wouldn't know what to do with one if she ever came into your life. For this reason alone, I will allow you to stay but you must stay where the servants stay. Perhaps then you will appreciate how well you've had it since your birth."

"Thank you, Father," Gaither said as he raised his head to see the king's disdain. "I will do as you say and learn to be more appreciative."

One evening, many months later, there was a terrible storm, thunder and lightning, and the rain poured down in torrents. Suddenly, a knocking was heard at the palace gate. The gatekeeper opened it and was surprised at what he saw. A princess was standing in front of the gate. The rain and the wind had made her look like a homeless waif. The water dripped from her hair and clothing. Her shoes were drenched as water poured from them and squished with every step.

"I have come from afar," she said as the gatekeeper listened. "I am in search of a real prince, a man who I have heard was in search of me. A real prince who is kind, understanding, loyal, and knows the worth of his caregivers as well as his own worth. Does a prince of this description reside here? If so, I am the real princess he has long searched for. I am Princess Julienne of the Castello Kingdom in Scotland."

"Follow me," the gatekeeper said as he led the princess into the courtyard and then to the palace. "Stand here," he said as he walked away leaving her dripping onto the white marble floors. "King Larriett," the gatekeeper called out while knocking on the huge wooden door leading into the King's bed chambers. "There's a young woman here who claims to be a real princess. She isn't quite the beautiful princess one might have expected but once she is out of her wet clothes and into something more princess appropriate, I believe she might be quite lovely. Sir, if you would please come and speak to her. I feel she is a bit confused as the prince she described seems nothing like Gaither, but I'll let you decide that."

King Larriett went to speak to the young woman.

"So, you say you are a real princess," he began, "We'll soon see if you speak the truth. I'll have a chambermaid see to your needs and find you clothing to wear. I'll be in and end any doubts I might have that you are telling a falsehood."

The King walked away as the chambermaid led Princess Julienne to her own bed chamber. Julienne was bathed and lotioned with the finest oils in the kingdom. Her hair was washed then braided with yellow ribbons streaming through out each braid.

Soon the King returned and knocked upon her door. "I have devised just the thing to insure you are a real princess." He led Princess Julienne to another bed chamber not as adorned as the one she had been originally shown to. "You will sleep in this bed chamber," he said. "One befitting the real princess you claim to be. The real test will be completed when tomorrow's light shines upon us. Good night for now."

The King walked away knowing the test he had laid out would confirm what he was hoping for in the back of his mind. This young woman was indeed quite stunning and just might be the real princess he had hope would one day adorn his Kingdom since the Queen's death.

The princess was exhausted as she fought her way onto the huge bed with the mattresses stacked almost to her neck.

The next morning the princess was asked how she had slept.

"Not well at all," said she. "I barely slept a wink. I have no idea what was on that bed but it was very hard. I feel as if I'm bruised from head to toe. I truly hate to complain but I had a terrible night."

The King now knew that she was a real princess because she had felt the pea through the twenty mattresses and the twenty eider-down beds he had his valet prepare her bed with.

"No one but a real princess could have been as sensitive as that," he proclaimed. The King refused to allow his son have this lovely creature because he was so undeserving of a lady of this merit. When the King asked her for her hand in marriage, she walked onto the balcony from his bed chamber and looked across the Kingdom and without hesitation she said, "yes."

She, too, had learned many wonderful tricks while on her journey to the Royal Bainbridge Kingdom. The King was soon at her beck and call as her sexual prowess seemed to fill him with the youthful zest he had long forgotten existed.

"My love," he would call out as he held his hand out to her for his weekly roust.

"I am yours," she would say removing her gown before throwing herself across the massive bed.

The King kissed her lips while stroking and probing her luscious thighs before diving deeply into her soul.

Their love making never grew tiresome as she brought new life to a King who had long forgotten what it felt like to be with real royalty again. She would never be his princess but instead his real queen and the deserving one to eventually take over the Kingdom.

Poor Prince Gaither remained at the palace for many years but never became the son his father desired. When he grew weary of watching the king and his new queen having such fun while he dressed in rags, he left, steering his stallion toward the home of the delightful Gwenevive. In her bed, he would find comfort and learn many new things.

All was well once again with the Royal Bainbridge family.

15

Master Vampire's Payback

Emil Stern

Year 1785

"Elder Yu? Here?"
(pause)
"Where is Master Kilmeade?"

Darcy's deep voice jostled Jersey from sleep. They had been keeping odd hours the past two weeks as Elder Kilmeade rotated his fellow Elders through the estate. Officially, they were attending business of the Fathers; unofficially, Jersey's master was showing off his dual fix-it men.

"Jerz, come on," Darcy said closer.

Still groggy, Jersey opened his eyes. In the back of his mind, a feather tickled as the unfamiliar Elder approached. He'd learned early on that when the Elders were near, his subconscious knew before his natural senses. Jersey attempted to rise, but his brain longed to sleep. He allowed a soft moan and succumbed, slipping back to the covers. The next sensation he knew was being violently jerked from his bed. Without a word or vocal admonishment, Jersey was shaken so furiously that his head swam. When he opened his eyes, he stared directly into Elder Yu's snarling face.

"Master!" Jersey focused, bringing his body online. Yu was incensed, his ire directed wholly to the man in his vicious grip. In the periphery, Darcy stood at attention, soldier-style, lined up with Kilmeade's captains, but Jersey did not look away from the Elder's red gaze. "I am your servant; whatever I have is yours," he rasped, aware he was moments away from severe punishment, his behavior greatly offending his master.

Yu was glorious and no other word—in any language—could possibly describe him. He towered over any man in the room, even Darcy, and if his height wasn't enough, his presence filled Jersey's consciousness as if not another person existed but himself and the god holding him inches off the ground.

"Oh, if I could please him, if only I could make him proud," Jersey's heart cried out, the interior workings of the Rakum unafraid of pain and the ish-mikhan spirit unafraid of appearing weak.

Yu lifted him over his head, spun him 180-degrees to drop him hard to the stone floor, Jersey's upper back absorbing the concussion with a snap of his scapula. The pain registered as a miniscule distraction as his vision cleared and he sought another view of Yu's face, now in profile as he shouted commands to the others in Rakum Hungarian.

"Oh, you are perfect, and I will show you… I am able to make you smile…" Jersey's heart continued to sing the Elder's praises and he lay still, his fractured bones healing with an itching tug. Yu swiveled his gaze and locked black eyes with Jersey's, still incensed.

He's angry with Kilmeade.

Jersey was unable to stop such thoughts, which trickled into his mind because of his predisposition to serve Elders. None of this eased Yu's hotly directed fury.

"If you like my thoughts so very much, have this one!" he barked in their language, bending low and because of his sheer size, appearing as if he moved in half-time to grasp Jersey about the throat. Jersey saw in his mind that the Elder wished him broken, *utterly*.

Kilmeade has stolen away his mate.

Another intuited thought slipped by and then—

No, she left Yu in preference to Kilmeade.

"Enough!" the master barked aloud and in his mind. Yu then shoved Jersey's body against the stone wall with all his might.

Jersey's vision blurred and he blinked out.

When he swam back, warm hands, supportive and healing, covered his wounds. He had only been out a few seconds. Elder Yu stood over him, seething, but Darcy was now at Jersey's side, his aroma as familiar as Jersey's own. His compatriot touched his cheeks with both hands—

Wait… then who's healing me?

Jersey lifted his gaze and over his left shoulder, he caught a tiny glimpse of auburn hair, soft waves that fluttered out of view, his master furiously repairing what Yu had broken. Kilmeade was in the habit of suppressing his body scent and in the melee Jersey had forgotten. Within another minute, every injury had been repaired and Kilmeade tenderly lifted Jersey to his feet.

"Elder Yu." Kilmeade spoke the name in a stern but quiet tone. "Welcome to my home." Jersey avoided Yu's eye recognizing that Kilmeade was reprimanding his fellow Elder. "Leave us," he continued in the same voice. "Ish-mikhan, remain."

The grunts and soldiers of both masters filed out. Darcy stood and moved to the wall near the door, awaiting a command, his eyes cast aside. Kilmeade's hands cupped Jersey's shoulders from behind and he ran one palm to his throat and stroked tenderly.

"You make me so proud," he sent privately and kissed the back of his ear with soft lips. To their guest, Kilmeade said in their language, "How do you find my ish-mikhan? Hardy, isn't he?"

It had been more a statement than a question and Jersey peeked for the Elder's response. His eyebrow fluttered, his lip curled, and then he relaxed his shoulders. Kilmeade had perhaps been speaking to Yu privately and Jersey pretended he didn't notice. Of course, both Elders caught his sentiment.

"Darcy," Kilmeade said, "show Master Yu to his quarters."

Jersey sighed and tried to hide it. Yu would prefer Darcy anyway—he was huge and just as capable of fixing the convolutions that ruined the Elder's mood tonight.

The two exited without a word or glance and when they were gone, Kilmeade turned Jersey in his grasp.

"You are an amazing seer, my pet, but you missed with Elder Yu." Kilmeade's gray eyes shone with affection and he kissed Jersey's mouth, hot and lingering. Jersey's respirations hyped, prepared to switch on and Kilmeade pulled back to see his face. "Yes, I took Yu's mate, but no, he doesn't prefer Darcy over you."

Jersey wondered at his words and Kilmeade kissed him again, sending silently, *"He raced me here tonight, sabotaged my mount so I had to run on foot. He wanted to ravish you and I forbid it. The best he could do before I arrived was break you a little…"*

"But he doesn't have to resist—if he wants me dead even, his will—" Jersey said in a low voice.

Kilmeade cut him off. *"No one does anything against what is mine. I allowed him to break you—as payback for little Jasmine, but none of them can best me in any capacity."*

Jersey said nothing. He had decided years ago that Kilmeade was their greatest Elder. Apparently, a goliath such as Yu recognized the same thing.

"Let him fuck Darcy. He does not deserve you—Kilmeade's first pup." Kilmeade gave him a devilish smile. *"Never forget your status. This title will follow you your entire life. You have earned it and you will always be my beloved favorite pet."*

Several rooms away, in the direction of the guest quarters, a loud crash sounded, reverberating the wall, before the house fell silent.

Kilmeade tweaked one eyebrow and then showed Jersey his pointer finger. *"Wait for it…"* he sent, his eyes to the side and sounds of pleasure followed. "Yu is fixed," he said aloud and dropped his hands to cross them at his chest. "Now, I have an itch."

"I will scratch it for you, Master," Jersey said low and Kilmeade grinned.

Excerpted from Blood, Sex & Violence, A Vampire's Rebuttal, *by Emil Jersey, Run Rabbit Books, 2019. www.emiljersey.com*

16

Going Human

Emil Stern

2017

Shirtless and relaxing alongside Avi on the couch, Jersey rubbed his belly in an absent manner, eyes on the television. Winston had pulled up a horror movie and for the moment, the nude teenagers on the cement floor hadn't noticed the monster bugs in the shadows. He and his brethren had fed well, locating a transient behind the burned-out paper mill, and now they sipped beers, full and comfortable, awaiting the sun. *Three hours until sunup,* Jersey counted inside, as every Rakum (ancient vampire race) knew at a cellular level where the sun sat on its track.

Still rubbing his middle, enjoying the tickle of the hair to his palm, Jersey flicked his eye to Win. The brother sat in a recliner cattycorner to he and Avi on the sofa, his face to the TV. Onscreen, a mutant insect crawled into the breasty teen's hair as her boyfriend rammed into her with gusto. Jersey watched her nipples, his mind wandering to the last woman he fucked as his own hand fell still. The Cows were gone, but females still found him beautiful. If he fancied a pussycat, he knew where to find one. Presently, Avi's left palm assumed the task of rubbing Jersey's stomach in similar circles and Jersey grinned without turning. Avi preferred men and Win would fuck a cantaloupe—anything moist inside suited his tastes. Once on a bet, he'd seen Win screw a horse. Jersey pivoted his eyes to Winston's profile. When it came to sex the biggest difference between the three of them was only Jersey refused to force sex. He didn't mind if they raped the entire city, but why do something he didn't want to do? He had no master. Part of their shitty new existence meant each man was on his own.

"That's a good boy, gooooooood boy," Avi cooed, moving his gentle and rhythmic stroking toward Jersey's waistband. He allowed the fingers to intermittently break the barrier and come back out toward his sternum. Jersey gave him a wink and looked back to the screen.

Winston turned at their movement. "Watch the movie, shit!" he hissed and faced front again.

Avi instead rolled onto his left which made petting easier. He put more ardor into each pass and leaned close to bury his face in Jersey's neck. "Let's go to bed, baby doll," he whispered between soft kisses.

Jersey still faced the movie and a scream erupted as a horde of alien roaches covered the woman's tits and she disappeared. The young man with her was saved the embarrassment of showing his junk eaten up by bugs as the camera panned away, on to the next scene. Avi had worked his mass in front of Jersey's right shoulder so Jersey brought that arm to rest around his brother's upper back. Winston looked at them again and gained his feet. He stomped to the couch and looked upon Jersey, hands to his hips.

"You requested this idiotic movie," he drawled with

a thumb to the television. "If you're gonna fuck anyone, it's gonna be me. It's my turn, Avi, and I will break you in two if you try to jump the line."

Avi did not lift his face from Jersey's jaw and said against his skin, "Chill out. I'm only getting him primed up for you."

Jersey grinned, it was a good game having his roommates focus their energy on him. He watched for Win's reaction. With a slow blink and a twitch in his cheek, Win turned away for the basement.

"I'm hitting the shower. And Jerz, you sure as fuck better be down there in seven minutes. Got it?" He left without a reply.

Jersey would go—it was their game. He loved being adored and even though they could all sleep together—and they had—sometimes it was nice to be singularly attended.

"I thought he'd never leave," Avi said in his throat, now slurping his tongue around Jersey's earlobe. They had lived together two years and his brethren had learned his buttons. Jersey's right palm sat quiet against Avi's shoulder blades and he rest his left flat to the cushion. Let Avi do all the work, it was his turn anyway.

The shower went on in the basement where they would sleep the day away from the sun. If he was headed down, he needed to go. Reading his surface thoughts, Avi rolled even more over his left and draped his right leg across Jersey's thighs.

"Let's piss him off," he said low in Jersey's ear. Without asking, his fingers unbuckled Jersey's belt and began with the button. "We can end this night in an all-out brawl."

"Sounds good," Jersey whispered, now closing his eyes and Avi went to work lower, perfection in his every suckle, squeeze, and lave. His brother made a sudden change in the play by hopping up to straddle Jersey and look him in the face.

"Let's make this work," he said in Jersey's eye, and with a mischievous grin he thrust his pelvis once. Jersey smiled too and his brother swooped in to lock their mouths.

Then the universe flipped upside down.

Jersey flushed from his forehead to his toes in a cascading wave of nausea, jerking backward into the sofa cushion, his actions unintentionally knocking Avi to the floor. The room grew darker and the television brighter as a heavy stone grew where Jersey normally felt his stomach. It was fifteen long seconds before he gathered his wits enough to look at his brother on the floor. Avi's eyes were enormous.

"What the shit?" Avi hissed. Shaking hands palpated his own chest, his face, and then he propped onto his knees to shove a hand down his pants and examine his genitals. "What's wrong with me? Say something. I think I'm going deaf!" Avi inhaled, his fear evident.

Fear? SHIT!

Jersey shook his head in a tiny movement and pressed his palms to his body in a similar manner. The answer to Avi's question whispered across his subconscious and he screamed inside, *No way. No way. No way. No…fucking…way…* When their third brother shouted, "WHAT THE FUCK!" in the basement, Jersey stood tucking his ruined erection into his jeans and re-securing his belt. When he turned for the hall, he halted after one step. His body felt heavy, as if he'd donned a suit of armor. He forced another step, and then another, and behind him Avi followed posing his questions to the air.

"Shut up, Avi! Just SHUT UP!" Jersey belted aware

that he had not yelled at either brother in anger since they met.

Anger? SHIT!

Stark naked and dripping water, Winston approached as they reached the basement floor. He met Avi's and then Jersey's eye, shaking his head side to side.

"No way," their brother said and reached Jersey to put a hand to his chest. Win cupped, squeezed, and prodded the muscle of Jersey's upper body and then his own, still mouthing, "no way."

"What? What is it?" Avi said in a high-pitched voice. "What's happening?"

Jersey put his hands to Winston's body and in a similar manner, rotated around to examine the broad surfaces of his muscled back.

"What? Judas Priest!" Avi said, near panic.

Panic? SHIT!

Fear, anger, panic – his inner mind listed off emotions, emotions Rakum did not possess.

"We're mortal," Jersey said in a very small voice his eye coming to rest in Winston's. "Fucking mortal."

"Mortal," Winston said just as low, holding Jersey's gaze with ferocity. Avi began to screech, exclaiming there must be another explanation, but Jersey and Win had no doubt.

"What do we do? What do we do? Who did this? WHAT THE SHIT IS GOING ON?" Avi's queries crescendoed and Winston clocked his jaw with a vicious right hook.

"Shut your hole, Avi, or I'll smash your face in!" he barked standing over his brother.

Avi had landed on his back and he remained there, eyes trained to the dark ceiling where a single bulb threw 40 watts of light across the basement. Blood ran from the side of his mouth—it wasn't red, but it also wasn't

Rakum-black.

Winston lifted his fist, rotated it to see his knuckles. The skin split over the first and second joint, seeping a similar half-n-half fluid from the wound. Jersey stepped into him and taking the hand in his fingers, lifted the blood to his lips. He tasted it and when it had rolled around his palate a few seconds, Win tasted it too.

"What?" Avi said in a whisper, his fingers smudging the trickle on his face and then bringing the sample to his tongue.

Jersey's bloodlust had disappeared; he knew it down to his deepest parts. The metallic flavor of his brother's blood should have at least tickled his hunger, but nothing happened. From his housemates' expressions, they sensed the same thing.

"Winston," Avi said then, using a voice they had only heard in mortals. A sound of terror and impending death.

Win looked to Jersey. "You're the master," he whispered, piling the responsibility upon the oldest among them. "Now what?"

Jersey held his eye three long seconds, his mind as clear as ever, his memory as sharp, his intellect intact. They all knew of brethren who had turned mortal on purpose, accepting the yoke the Rabbit Beth Rider offered them at Last Assembly, but it had been voluntary. Why had the three of them turned human at such a random moment?

Jersey blinked and put a comforting palm to Win's shoulder. The sun was upon them, the house upstairs locked down. For the next eight hours, he and his two brothers would hash it out, phone Rakum they knew, get to the bottom of the issue. Jersey put out a hand to Avi and jerked him to his feet. By sundown, they'd have an answer, and if Avi could keep his cool, they wouldn't have to kill him before then. First order of business? Jersey brought both men close with his arms across their shoulders. It was mortal. It was a hug. But somehow, it gave them courage to face what lay ahead.

FETISH | Bonus Novelette

The most beautiful woman in the world said I was perfect. To a feckless, rudderless kid with half of his face grotesquely missing, the compliment is nearly enough to convince me to sell my soul. Notice I said nearly…

It's not a fetish, geez! It's not like I rub women's gloves on my privates. You're coming at this all wrong. Listen to my story, you'll see. It's not a fetish, dammit. This is how it went.

We were having one of those monsoons; not like

they have in Bangladesh, but like we have on the mountain in North Alabama, at the ass-end of the Appalachians, when summer and fall clash, fight, and do their best to kill us with tornados and hail. My aunt's rain gauge read three inches already, so for me, it would be a weary night of checking the basement for leaks every hour upon the hour.

Now, to the woman.

She came in dripping wet

and when I rushed at her with a towel, she winced as if I'd threatened her with a machete. Or, more likely, she shrunk away because of my surgical mask.

"Oh!" she exclaimed, arms out, gloved fingers open, ready to receive the cloth. "Thank you. Wow! It's really coming down out there!"

The woman first touched the fabric to her face, one cheek–*pat-pat-pat*—and the other. Daubed her lips, careful, I thought, to not smudge her lipstick, then her forehead, just a little swab. Then she patted her graceful neck, turning her chin left and then right, my eyes following—oh, what a beautiful throat she had. That done, she lowered her gaze to consider the water on her clothing. I watched her hand go to her sternum and head down, the palm slipping over the curve of her right breast, to her flat middle and coming to a stop on the rise of her hip. She raised her eyes to mine.

"Not too bad, considering," she said, her voice soft. I stepped back to give her room and she gave me a smile. "Not too bad at all."

I smiled back, but she would only see my eyes crinkle, my mask bunching upward with the movement. I gestured that she should come in and pondered everything about her. Easily the most beautiful woman I had ever seen, this lady was covered neck-to-foot in a stretchy, white lace garment lined with creamy silk. It hugged her perfect upper body, sliding down her toned arms to end at her delicate wrists. There, it tucked into slim white leather gloves.

I ogled on and, so far, she didn't mind. She arched her back, suddenly needing a stretch. I watched her chest, round, each breast the size of a man's hand. *My hand,* to be specific. And, was she wearing a onesie? At her waist, the lacey clothing became a pantsuit that reached her ankles and ended in short high-heeled boots. You'd think she was some sort of flagrant floozy in such a get-up, but if you saw her face, you'd say she was an angel. I mean, she wore the softest expression, as if she had never raised her voice in anger; so different from my aunt who spent every day worrying and griping, and the hostel boarders who hated my deformity even though none had ever seen it up close.

Yes, our new guest might have truly come from heaven—if that part is real—I can't say, I haven't died yet.

She didn't wear makeup except for on her lips. They glossed with a pink schmeer that was probably tasty, you know, flavored, like teenie-boppers use (I'm guessing they use it, based upon television commercials).

Our guest's wet hair had been worn off her neck, twisted against her head, affixed with sparkling jewel-studded barrettes. I guessed it would reach her waist when down. I'd always been a sucker for long-haired blondes. (That's a funny thing to write when I've never had a girlfriend. I guess I never will; this face is a great repellant.)

She didn't carry a purse and wore a gold necklace with various unfamiliar sigils attached, charm-style. The woman intrigued me beyond words, and when Aunt Edna entered the foyer to welcome the newcomers, I stepped backward to lean against the stair railing and watch her check in. Was she alone? It would be a near impossibility. She'd left the door ajar as if someone would follow directly. I sighed, my hot breath—thankfully minty since I just brushed—warming my lower face and cooling just as quickly.

"Heavens!" Aunt Edna exclaimed then, moving into our guest's space to retrieve the towel and hand her a new one. "Get in here, child! We got to get you dry! You'll catch your death of cold!"

My aunt used her body position to usher the woman to the registration desk. I remained in place, watching, listening and expecting a burly and handsome husband to come in from the rain any moment carrying the beauty's luggage.

Fifteen feet away, Edna took down the woman's information. Her name was Roxanne Siren, and it was her brother (*not husband, wink-wink*) who wrestled the luggage outside.

I left the stairs to peek through the front door's glass inserts. Sure enough, a shortish, bald gentleman with no hat nor umbrella was scooting through the drenching thunderstorm, toting two medium-sized bags. I shoved the door open the rest of the way and viewed the couple's Volvo through the sheeting rain. It looked new but the right front tire sported a may-pop, which might explain why this fancy couple pulled into our broken-down bed and breakfast in the first place.

We were right off the interstate on a long strip of no hotels and no gas stations. In 1890, the house sat alone on two hundred acres. In 2020, Edna owned only the three acres around the structure. A few house trailers had moved close, but so far, modern business avoided this end of the county.

"Dammit!" the guy hissed as he neared,

pronouncing the curse as, "*dahh*-mitt". I made way as he jumped onto the porch only to stop before me and meet my eye.

"Good evening, sir," he said in a European accent. "May I come in, please?"

I didn't reply—was he for real? It's a bed and breakfast, guy, read the sign. But he waited for me to answer, his expression unchanging. I threw him a bone. He had an accent; maybe he was a foreigner and didn't know better.

I made a smirk he wouldn't see because of my mask and gestured for the foyer. "Please, come in."

Baldy sent me a pert nod, and after narrowing his eyes a split-second at my face, he slipped in, dripping a trail of water behind. Overcome with a rare sense of propriety, I pointed him toward reception.

"Right through there. Aunt Edna will get you checked in."

He said thank you and sloshed away. I studied him as he reached his sister. He wasn't tall and he carried weight around the middle—the sort that comes from donuts, not beer. That made me smile and I resumed my spying stance by the staircase. Then what I hate the most happened—my nose tickled. I don't have allergies, but now and then, dust can make me sneeze. *Sneezing* causes me to remove my mask.

To avoid drawing the new folks' eyes, I turned my back and lifted the fabric just in time. *"Ah-CHOO!"*

Then, my mask back in place, I turned to see the woman, Roxanne, looking my way. I blushed, she smiled, and then faced my aunt again.

I'm so glad she can't see what I'm hiding.

It's gruesome. At age twelve, my face was horribly disfigured in a car crash. How, you ask? In short, it came clean off—from an inch below my hairline to the start of my chin, the flappy surface on the front of my head was sheared sideways by sharp metal flashing in the collision. A quick-thinking First Responder lifted it from its skewed position and put it more or less back in place, wrapped my head with gauze, and airlifted me to the city hospital.

Did it hurt? No. I can't remember feeling any pain before, during, or after the crash. The pain arrived the next morning when I awoke—my face re-affixed and my parents, dead.

The doctor came in that morning to tell me what he and his team worked on through the night in order for me to be able to eat, breathe, and speak after such a catastrophic injury. A team of eleven physicians and nurses reattached my nose, reconstructed my lips (which they built from skin harvested from my caboose), re-settled my eyeballs, and re-structured my jaw which had broken in two places.

All this diligent medical assistance left me with a monster's visage, a mutant's punim, a maniac's façade. Combine my surgical scars, of which there are many, with my pasty complexion and a struggling five o'clock shadow that I can't keep mowed because my follicles are still in shock, I was an *ugly* specimen. I don a surgical mask for the comfort of the populace.

I suppose I should be thankful that my eyes look normal and the furrow scar in my forehead is easily disguised by leaving my shaggy brown hair long and floppy up top.

But it's lonely. After the accident, my personality changed (that's what the child psychologist said, anyway) and I chased off my old friends with my new sour disposition. Since then, six years have passed and making new pals has so far proven to be an impossibility. Aunt Edna allowed me to move in as soon as I was discharged from the hospital and I live upstairs in one of her rooms. I don't go out much and she lets me do odd jobs that don't include interacting with her guests.

I will be nineteen in a week and I wish I was dead. That about sums up my existence.

"Billy, please take these bags up to Room 4," Edna called and I huffed.

She had a habit of treating me as if I was the most normal kid in the world, as if I wasn't scarier to look at than the worst horror movie demon.

I did as she asked and walked around the dividing half-wall to make a grab for Baldy's suitcases. I clutched one, but he snatched the other out of reach before I could grasp it.

"I have this one, son, thank you," he said without looking up. The Gloved One turned at his hissing tone and gave me a smile that I felt somewhere south of my belt buckle.

"Jasper, you're so cranky," she said to her brother, playfully slapping the air toward him, her eyes in mine. She sidled toward me and reached out as if to touch my floppy hair. Jasper grunted and she lowered her hand. "He's so grumpy," she said to me as Jasper came between us and forced us apart.

I didn't say anything, my mind still playing over the woman's every movement, every word. She mesmerized me, tantalized me, intrigued, and confused me. I wish she had touched my hair.

When I was eleven, Mom hired a cook. She and Dad were attorneys and they got tired of doing some of the mundane housework themselves. After the cook, next came a maid, and by the time they settled on a full staff, I had a chef all to myself. Tania Tucker. She was old, probably fifty, but she had long blonde hair that she wore in a ponytail down her back. I used to reach for it and fondle it in my hand when she stirred my lunch on the stove. My favorite memory of Tania was one I never told anyone.

It was the Friday my parents had to work late and they asked Tania to stay and keep me from mischief. The rest of the staff went on home and Tania fed me my favorite meal—spaghetti and meatballs. Over dinner, she sat across from me and made me laugh. I never considered her fun to talk to until that night. She allowed me to follow her around since she was hired, but I only did that because Mom said she was mine.

"Tania is your chef, Bill. All yours. Whatever you want to eat, you only have to ask, okay?"

Tania was mine, so from age eleven to the time of the crash, I considered her my servant. Hey, I was a kid. Cut me some slack.

Anyway, after we ate, she invited me to watch cartoons with her in the grownup's den. I didn't go in there, it's where Mom and Dad met with guests and smoked and laughed and drank alcohol. Now I sat in there with my cook, and she positioned us in the center of the sofa looking at an enormous flatscreen television. She patted her thighs and I sat on her lap, facing forward. Heck, I didn't care. My stomach was full to capacity and her legs and belly were soft. Her lap was superior to the couch cushion in every way.

Once I was settled, she let her hair down. Good god, I loved her hair. I asked her to drape it over my shoulders and said I'd pretend it was my hair. She giggled and I leaned back into her chest, my legs atop hers, both of us facing the television, and she parted her locks evenly over each of my shoulders. It hung to my middle and I stroked it as she set the volume on the TV. The next thing she did is what made my night (and maybe my life). I heard a strange noise and smelled latex, and she set gloved hands to my thighs on either side. I watched the TV and her palms slid up and down, humming a soft tune, as if comforting a frightened doggie. My body began to tingle. On the screen, a rabbit ran from a Tasmanian devil and Tania hummed. My middle thrummed. Tania stroked, and my crotch felt bunched and tight. This went on a little while until the weirdest feeling I ever had in my life shot through my body. When the shivering ceased, I laughed. I looked at my lap and saw those purple house gloves on my legs and that long blonde hair curling on either side of my chest and said, "Dang, that was weird!"

Tania giggled and wrapped me into a hug, putting her chin over my shoulder, and we watched the end of the show. When the credits ran and a new show began, I asked her to rub my legs again with those gloves. She worked for me, you know, so she obliged. I can't tell you what we were watching, and I don't remember when Mom and Dad got in, but I remember those gloves and her beautiful, beautiful hair.

Roxanne put her gloved hand to her lips just then and I refocused. I had been looking into her eyes when my mind wandered off. Now, she was smiling a secret grin, and she gave me a "shush" gesture combined with a wink. I looked away. What was that?

Edna stepped around the woman blocking my view. "Okay, but I'm afraid you've missed dinner. Breakfast is served from six to eight, and then lunch from eleven to one. Food in the yellow fridge is for the guests, the silver one is off limits, okay dearies?" Edna looked to the strangers' faces. When no one answered, she put down her pen and managed to catch the Gloved One's eye. "I just wanted you to know because the last guests who came to dinner late missed the chicken. It was awful, they had to subsist on leftover meatloaf. You don't want that to happen to you, eh?"

I grimaced, embarrassed at an old woman's take on mealtimes; not everyone lived and breathed scheduled feed-bagging. Jasper was already to the first stair and he shook his head.

"Thank you, ma'am, but no need for meals; we brought our own food. Come along, Roxanne."

With that, he shuffled up the steps carrying the obviously heavier of the two bags. The woman sent me a flirtatious wink and followed him, and after two strides, I tailed her to the landing. After I'd directed them to the correct room and set down the black suitcase, Jasper stepped between Roxanne and me and held out a fiver. A tip? I didn't have anything to spend it on; Edna gave me a credit card to use online. And what could I get with five bucks? I collected shot glasses, guess that might buy a single addition. I tucked the bill in my pocket, and left the room.

As the door was closing, I glanced backward, hoping to get another look at the gloved beauty queen, and witnessed something odd. Roxanne raised her arms in the surrender position and Jasper moved toward at double-speed. Then, the door slammed as if shoved by an invisible force, right in my curious face.

I remained in place, listening for a cry for help, but no one screamed. No one cried. No one said anything. After a few seconds, I stepped away from the door and heard an exhale. It was loud and throaty, more feminine than masculine. Call me Mr. Diligent because I made an about-face and entered Room 3. Somebody had to keep an eye on these two.

It rained through the night, and in the morning the front yard had become a pond. Guests sloshed through two inches of standing water to get to the sidewalk and there was nothing sweet Edna could do about it. I didn't like yardwork and she did the landscaping herself. I didn't like to sweat, it actually hurt the skin of my face, to be honest. My scars are stretched tight and maybe it's psychological, but I sometimes think my cheeks might split open. Sometimes I dream my face fell off in the night. I sit up, look over, and it's on the rug looking up at me. But not last night.

Last night, I dreamed about Roxanne.

Dream Roxanne wore purple latex gloves and snuck into my room as I slept. She crawled under the covers and I awoke to her caressing my scarred cheek with one gloved hand. She looked into my eyes and told me I was handsome. She ran her gloved finger along my re-created bottom lip and said she wanted to kiss me there, long and gentle. In real life, I hadn't kissed a girl, but a man has the internet, which meant I mostly wanted to see my dream girl naked. In a blink, she was nude. I'm not sure what she came to bed in, but she wore nothing now.

Dream Billy reached blindly toward her torso under the sheet, looking into her liquid eyes, my room lit only by the moon in the open window. Dream Billy's fingers prodded, examined, and traveled along her body until I found what might have been a nipple. She didn't object so I sought the other one, found it, and she encouraged me with a new kiss. Did I dare go lower? Hell, it was my dream, so I did. My top hand slid along her silky skin and found her abdomen. She sighed and rolled onto her back, languid and cat-like, stretching her arms above her to the headboard, arching her back. The sheet traveled down a few inches as she did so and her glorious chest blinded me with its beauty. My hand was out of sight, sitting at her navel, under the sheet. Dare I go farther? Dare I?

But I couldn't.

Stupid dream. Curse it!

My hand wouldn't move. It hovered there, her tummy rising and falling, my hand riding along with the movement, and I could *not* go lower. I woke up sweating, angry and sad altogether.

And it was still raining when I clopped down the stairs in my joggers and T-shirt, plus of course, my mask. It was almost three o'clock, and the impromptu swimming pool created in the front had drained to the back.

Where was my girlfriend?

The Gloved One and her rude brother had not made a peep. I had remained in Room 3 until Edna chased me out at midnight. Then, from my own room which faced the street, I watched to see who came and went. As the man had indicated, Roxanne and Jasper did not come to breakfast or lunch. I was increasingly suspicious that the guy had killed her. (Side note: an active imagination and a freakazoid face are always a two-for-one deal.)

At 3:30, FM100 interrupted a Beatles marathon to announce a manhunt underway for the murderer of three college freshman. They'd been found dead of apparent heart attack in the Mill Town Historical Park. The police didn't think it was possible that all three could die the same way at the same time and determined it must be homicide.

Uh, duh. Good call. Mill Town Police, people. Can we get a round of applause?

The announcer said similar killings had occurred in several states, leaving a trail from California to the

Carolinas of unusually-young myocardial infarction victims.

A serial killer? In Mill Town? Then again, why not? it had to happen in someone's town. I sometimes studied criminals, their autobiographies and TV documentaries. I liked to pretend I could do that, end someone's life and get off on it. Get sexually aroused by watching someone's eyes dilate as they left this mortal plane. But I fooled myself. I grew physically ill at the notion of blood, much less seeing it. I had a low threshold for pain and found it too easy to vomit when things got stressful. This last issue was what landed me in the therapist's office after my last facial surgery.

Before I ran off my very last friend, I missed school and couldn't concentrate when I went. I couldn't meet the teacher's eye and assumed every laugh and giggle was about my deformity. At thirteen, Aunt Edna found me one morning sleeping in my own vomit. She had helped me clean up, then driven me into town that same day. The hospital got me in to a therapist immediately and the man's first order of business was to hand me a little white mask to cover the lower half of my face. This was the beginning of my healing. I might not ever be the way I was before the crash, but with the mask on, *I can at least live.*

I was a superhero now. All I needed was a cape! And over the next few weeks, I chose my characteristics. Billy the Half-Face Wonder was a loner, he had telepathy, and was impervious to pain. I know I became a pain in the ass to my friends and teachers, but Edna stood by me. I got suspended the first time for spitting on the younger children as they passed my classroom door. The next year, I snuck into the younger kids' playroom while they slept and rolled them over as if they were dolls. I laugh now because when they caught me doing this weird behavior, they told Edna I was crazy, maybe dangerous. And they wanted to know why I wore the teacher's painting gloves when I did it. Edna asked me and I told her the truth—thirteen-year-old Billy liked the way they felt to my hands when I wore gloves. Children are mushy. I'd only touch their arm, and just… r-o-l-l him or her onto his back, or front, or whatever it took.

Anyway, after that suspension, Edna withdrew me from school and I finished my coursework at home. Hell, I had no plans for college. I guess then and now I assumed I'd stay with Edna until she died. I mean, what else can a man with my destroyed face expect?

But I digress…

At 4 p.m., I was again listening through the wall to Room 4 and Edna asked me to peel potatoes. I reluctantly left my post to do her bidding. Edna was even-tempered, but strict, too. Unlike the other two meals, dinner was served once at 6 o'clock sharp. When I reached the kitchen, she pointed to the sink where she'd left the potatoes, washed and ready to scrape. I went to it and out of the corner of my eye, Aunt Edna rubbed her eyes. Was she crying? I looked her way and she waved and left me alone.

I began the task thinking about Aunt Edna's tears. She had heartache, who wouldn't? My uncle left her with nothing, and she was advanced in age and had never worked. She was doing a great job with the bed and breakfast, sure, but she had no retirement. I heard her once on the phone with the bank—every penny she had was in the property. They didn't turn a profit, they broke even. Month after month. Year after year. She couldn't retire. Ever.

That was damn depressing and I shook my head and body to clear my mind. At least my aunt had

Valium. I stole one from her last year when I ran low of my prescription for Oxy. Aunt Edna got by on sleep and internal cheer. That would have to be good enough.

Finally!

When every potato in Alabama had been peeled, she released me to return to my spying. I journeyed up to still-vacant Room 3 to listen in. Lordy-lordy, this time, our guests were making noise.

"Uhhhhhhhhh, please, please...please..." The sultry female voice seeped through the wall, and once again, I felt an odd tightness in my gut and a longing below the belt. It was a sincere, begging plea; what could she possibly need that badly from her brother?

Drugs? Crap. The beautiful Miss Siren was an addict. No fair.

"Stop it!" a male voice hissed.

I recognized that tone as Jasper's.

"Put your gloves on! Right NOW!"

The second hiss was more audible, and furniture bumped the floor.

"Jasperrrrr, pleassssse...."

Gross. She was *purring.* Was something sexual going on in Room 4? She sounded seductive, not like someone jonesing for a hit.

The door to the hall opened and slammed closed, then heavy footsteps hurried down the stairs. To me, this means the Gloved One was alone and possibly horny. Did the Masked Mutant have a chance?

I left Room 3, and with my knuckles hovering over the brass number on Room 4, I took a deep breath. The door swung open before I knocked.

"Billy, isn't it?" she asked, standing with her hand on her hip.

Again, she was wrapped from her flawless neck to

her tiny ankles, this time in a soft green velour jumpsuit. Did I mention I love velour? Also, as before, she wore matching leather gloves and short boots. I'd been quiet too long and she motioned inside.

"Please, come in, Billy."

"Okay," I said like a moron. I plodded in, happy she couldn't see the quivering of my grotesque lips. Thankfully, my mask hid all sorts of unexpected emotional responses.

"Please, sit with me. Tell me about this town, this Bed and Breakfast, your aunt. Tell me why you wear that mask." She lighted in the room's only sofa, a decorative, scroll-y job with a rose pattern. That left the pink Queen Anne chair for me.

I sat stiffly, wondering which of her topics to tackle first. I would tell her anything just to watch her mouth move and have her eyes stare deep into mine—I'd sell my soul for an undisturbed hour alone with her.

She asked about the city and I started with the history of Mill Town, Alabama's largest small town. The country's oldest Fire Department dalmatian resided here. The mayor held eleven academic degrees—a world record for mayors. Our public-school system stopped using buses in 2009 and now the children walk to school in groups led by the former bus drivers. Crazy stuff like that, I let it all fly. Then I gave her the run-down on Edna's rocky past. The death of her wealthy husband who, because of lack of foresight and attention to detail, left his inheritance to his first wife. How when Edna thought she was about to go broke, my mother pitched in and helped her purchase the town's only B&B with cable and Wi-Fi. Aunt Edna had it tough, but she was a sturdy type—I was impressed by her optimism, and I said so.

About the time I got to my own story, Edna's voice

trickled up announcing dinner; I was supposed to help serve. I stood and Roxanne followed suit. Her hair was down, and I had guessed correctly—it was wavy and wheat blonde, reaching down her back to her waist.

"Wait," she said and took a step closer. "Wait…" she whispered the second time and lifted leather-wrapped fingers to my eye-level.

Oh, I wished those fingers would touch me.

"Wait, just a moment, *please*…"

Whispering again, and begging, as I'd heard through the wall earlier. My follicles reacted to the sensation of her touch as she moved my rascally curls aside and then stroked, once, twice, three times, without ever making true contact with my scalp. Why didn't matter, only that she didn't stop. At that moment, an insane phrase came out of my mouth.

"You can touch me, Roxanne. It's okay."

I stood only inches away and when the words left my mouth, a look crossed her face that I'd never before seen. Was it exhilaration? Joy? Perverse fear? I think it was all three.

Roxanne withdrew her fingers and right under my nose, I watched her slowly, no—*provocatively*—slip the glove from her hand. Her fingers appeared as if made of porcelain, fragile yet strong, with baby-pink polish perfectly applied to mid-length nails. The hand was getting closer. Oh, yes, she was about to touch me. I bent my knees a smidge so I wouldn't pass out.

"Billy," she breathed, inching in like they do when a man and woman are just about to kiss in the movies, "where should I touch you? Where will you allow it?"

I was supposed to choose? What did it matter? *Just do it!*

"Where should I touch you, Billy? Where?"

My tongue stuck to the roof of my mouth and I

wished I had telepathy. I'd tell her *touch me here and there and everywhere, you beautiful princess of heaven!*

Roxanne's manicured fingers moved toward my hairline and an electric buzz coursed to my head as if attracted by her touch. The instant her fingers made contact, she moaned a throaty sound. Her beautiful storm-blue eyes rolled up, her pink lips parted and I fell in love with her mouth.

Then…

I lost consciousness.

"So impetuous! You couldn't wait one more hour? One? Look at this! If you kill your prospects, you'll never be matched up!"

"You're overreacting. I have another one lined up."

"It's never a done-deal! You know this better than I do!"

Lying flat on my back, I didn't open my eyes as I came to, but I recognized the voices overhead.

"Dammit, your highness, they won't alter the moon for you again."

They won't alter the moon? That was a weird thing to say. What did he mean? The real moon was set in its orbit; did I miss-hear?

They won't alter *damoon.*

Da-moon.

That sounds like a noun, right? A city. A plan. *Alter a dress called damoon…*

"Hush, Jasper, watch your mouth. He's not dead."

He's not dead…

Did I look dead? I considered my extremities—I felt fine. I decided to listen in while Jasper released his frustrations on my new girlfriend.

"Thank goodness for that," he responded not as close as the woman. Then he sighed. "You just had to do it, didn't you? I'm afraid you'll get caught breaking the rules, that's all."

"They're my rules, anyway. You worry about nothing. And don't be mad. Look at him—he's perfect."

"He's deformed."

"No, he's perfect." Based on the direction of her voice, it was Roxanne's toe that touched my hip. "He's empathetic, intelligent, resilient, introverted; what else can a girl ask for?"

"You're not a girl and this kid is not worthy of you."

Rough hands grabbed me under the armpits and dragged me across the floor.

"Buzz the front desk. We'll say he fainted and we want him out of our room."

Jasper placed me on the rosy couch and he was none to gentle about it. Figuring it was time to awaken, I groaned and fluttered my eyelashes.

"See? He's fine…"

"Don't you touch him!" Jasper barked in a creepy hiss, then shouted, "PUT YOUR GLOVES BACK ON!"

I opened my eyes in time to see Roxanne playfully reach for Jasper's arm with her bare fingers. He jerked away, but she'd made the briefest contact. He fell to his knees, facing her, his profile to me.

She looked down on him and shook her pointer near his nose. "What's that Jasper? What do you want me to do? Where are my gloves? I don't remember…"

Jasper remained on his knees, looking into her face, apparently dazed. She tossed me a look and gave me a secret smile before putting her un-gloved hand to Jasper's face. That's when I noticed I wasn't wearing my mask.

"OHMYGOD!" I yelped, covering my scars with both hands. I hopped up and the Gloved One caressed her brother's cheek. He convulsed with what looked like pleasure. Feeling naked and confused, I screamed like a little girl and bolted from the room. The fact that Roxanne's fingers contained an unexplained power didn't register until I'd made it into my own room, locked the door, and tied on a new surgical mask.

He's deformed.

Ugh. Jasper said that about the plastic surgeon's nightmare that I call a face.

No, he's perfect.

Wait. Roxanne said that—whilst looking right into my sleeping monster visage. What else did she call me?

I busily worked to remember her every word as my last visual of her came to mind; her touch somehow incapacitated her brother. Is that why I fainted? She was reaching for my hair and the next thing I know, I'm on the floor.

Gloves, gloves, gloves... It's not a fetish, stop with that word.

Jasper said, "*You're not a girl...*"

Then what was she?

She couldn't wait one more hour?

For what?

In the fog that befuddled my senses, I heard the weighty front door slam. I sprinted to the window in my unlit room and looked down on the now-dark street. It must have been about 9 p.m. and the widely-spaced streetlights only allowed visual contact every dozen feet. The shadow that left the house at a good clip could have been anyone, but I wanted to think it was Jasper. I wanted him to have left in a huff, to have left the house for good, because that would mean Roxanne was alone, and she had said that I was *perfect.*

I left the room dark so I could continue my surveillance of the front yard. Before long, a soft knock caused me to jump. In the hallway, Aunt Edna asked if I was okay, reminding me that since I missed dinner, she had saved me a plate in the microwave. She sounded tired, as if running a bustling B&B practically on her own was wearing her out. I couldn't imagine how she'd made it this long. She was barely sixty, but looked ten years older, with smoker's lungs and one leg shorter than the other since her youth. She didn't spend a lot of time smiling.

At any rate, I called out that I was fine and she went away. She was good like that—letting me take care of my own business. A lot of guardians surprised by a sudden familial boarder would make life hell for their guest, but not Edna. It was her sister—my mom—that passed in the crash and since I moved in, she treated me like a nephew and that was all I asked.

I returned my gaze to the night below and scouted for movement. When I put my hands to the sill and leaned close enough for my covered nose to touch the glass, I sensed someone behind me.

"Billy?"

I yelped like an even younger girl than before and spun around. Roxanne stood a few paces behind me, illuminated only by the romantic light of the moon, her gloved hands at her sides, the shimmery green bodysuit complimenting her eyes. Who was this woman? How did she get in? What did she want? It really didn't matter if she was going to remove her gloves.

"Yeah? I'm sorry, I'm a dummy," I mumbled, and then said some other stupid things before her smile re-

tickled my insides.

"You said I could touch you. Did you mean it?"

She stood about five feet away. If we both put out our hands, we could touch fingers. I nodded and wondered just what I was agreeing to. Her hand on Jasper's cheek turned him to jelly; her fingers on my hair knocked me out cold.

"Good…" She took a tiny step forward and stopped. "Jasper didn't come through."

I was curious at her meaning, but my eyes went to her gloves. Was she going to touch me again? *Please, please.*

"It's his fault, isn't it, Billy? If he had checked the tires more often, we wouldn't have had a blowout, right?"

She wanted me to agree with her. I tried, but what came out was, "Unless he ran over some debris in the road. He couldn't help that."

Her heart-shaped mouth went to the side. "If that was the case, he should have been more vigilant when driving a princess across the country, right? A vigilant man watches for debris when the princess's welfare is in his hands."

Who knows? Wait, she's a princess?

"Maybe," I said hoping she'd come closer. Her touch knocked me out, but the pleasure explosion it caused was worth it.

"If he'd been more diligent, then I'd be with my match right now. I had him picked out, but the window was narrow before he was no longer available."

Roxanne moved a few inches closer until her face was washed in heavenly moonlight. Only one of us would have to reach out now in order to touch fingertips.

"Your match?" I asked, hearing her odd musings

as if from miles away. I was about twenty percent interested in what she was saying; the rest of me concentrated on her hands dangling at her sides. Any second now, she might lift one and…

"They're so hard to nail down," she said in a pout. "I located this one a week ago and Jasper promised he'd get me there in time."

Awwww, she looked forlorn. What could I do that would make her smile? I tried what had worked before.

"You can touch me, Roxanne. It's okay."

She beamed me with her famous smile and closed the distance between us. "Okay, I will. But first let me finish with Jasper."

"Whatever," I said aloud, not meaning to do so. I meant, *whatever so long as you touch me before I explode.*

Roxanne gestured to the night outside. "You should watch. It will mean more to you if you watch."

I turned and looked out the window, puzzling at her words. She hardly said anything that made sense, but I had a hard time caring. I scanned the dark silhouettes of the trees, the rooftops of the neighboring mobile homes, then the sidewalk below and finally detected movement in the street. It was a person, short of stature, with a shine to his bald head.

"I need you, Billy, to either be my Jasper or to be my match."

"I don't follow," I said, watching Jasper intently below. He stood in the middle of the road, facing the house, his details bathed in shadow. Cherry Lane was a back, back, back road; he needn't worry about traffic.

"Watch," she reiterated, close enough behind me that her breath fell on my neck.

Below, Jasper put his hands in his pockets, still staring in our direction. I made as if to lift my hand to wave when an eighteen-wheeler zoomed across my vision, mowing the man down in an instant. I yelped, but then Roxanne's gloved finger touched the top of my hand.

"I need you, Billy." The pressure increased where she touched me and the electricity between us sparked deep within. "Jasper's gone. It's up to you. Choose."

Choose? My brain didn't seem to be working properly; I'd just seen a man run down by a giant truck and all I could do was focus on the heat between her leather-encased finger and the top of my hand. Pinned as I was to the spot, a moan escaped my lips. Roxanne put two fingers atop my hand and pressed down.

"Choose, Billy. *Pleasssseeee…"*

Oh, she was begging again. *Yes, whatever, I'm yours, what do you want?* My mind went crazy with answers, but I didn't understand the question.

"I need you, Billy," she cooed, the opposite gloved hand coming to rest on my left shoulder. Instantly, a party raged there and tingles of pure ecstasy traveled down my spine to every extremity.

Yes, *every* extremity.

What if she removed her gloves? What then?

"Pleasssseeee choooooooose…"

I coughed, facing outside, but seeing nothing. My mouth asked an inane question. "Do you need to touch to live?"

Why did I ask that? I'm so stupid.

"Where's the gun?"

Huh? I'd never owned a gun, never held one. I fired a BB gun one Easter before the accident. My dad filled it with pellets and walked me to the yard to shoot stuff. I aimed at birds and squirrels, missed. I aimed at the fencepost, missed. I took aim at the side of the barn—heard a ping. That's it. That's my experience with firearms in that one afternoon with Dad. I looked over my shoulder and caught her eye. She fluttered her lashes.

"Where are the pills?"

Oh... That one hit a mark. In my bathroom drawer I had collected about a hundred prescription pills from dozens of guests over the past few months. Most of them were anti-depressants, and I figured they'd kill you if you took them all at once. One website said an overdose of Xanax brought on unconsciousness and if I mixed any of them with too many shots of whiskey, my brain would stop telling my lungs to breathe. Now and then, more often than I am willing to admit, I think about that forever-sleep. Roxanne was still looking into my face and I didn't want her to know I toyed with the idea of offing myself.

"Get them, Billy. Go get those pills. If you take them, you'll be my match."

Roxanne's voice was urgent and low. I read the eagerness in her eyes and wondered how my suicide could help either of us.

"What are you talking about? I don't want to die." I said whatever came to me.

Roxanne's face fell and she shrunk away, the tantalizing contact with her gloved fingers disappearing as she did so.

"Wait... You can touch me, Roxanne." I sounded like a pathetic broken record.

"Suicides match me, Billy. I thought you wanted me to touch you. What's the problem?"

Clearing steadily, my mind raced a mite faster than sludge.

"Let me see if I get this: Jasper was taking you to a man who you somehow knew was about to commit suicide and because of the blow out, you missed your window and the man is dead."

Roxanne nodded. "It hurts me not to touch. It hurts normal people when I do."

She glanced out the window. Down below red, white, and blue lights flashed as ambulances, police, and fire medics arrived to peel the dead man off Cherry Lane.

"Suicides, seized at the point of death, can be touched and live."

"That doesn't make sense," I sent back. "What kind of person kills people with their touch?"

"No kind of *person* does, Billy."

You're not a girl, and he's not worthy of you…

Jasper said that earlier. What did it mean?

"You're not a person?" I asked and tucked my hands under my armpits.

"Not like you are."

Roxanne removed her left glove and my stomach roiled, this time in a bad way. In my mind's eye, I saw dead college kids. I thought of the gloved creature's electric touch and was beginning to try out the kind of math where one plus one equaled two. "Did you kill those boys at the park?"

"Billy, pleeeease…." she cooed, her eyes sorrowful, her glistening lips begging me to surrender. "It hurts me *not* to touch. It *hurts* me."

"But why those kids? And why three of them?"

Was I the police now? I hated my questions because I didn't want to know the answers.

"Three, three hundred, three thousand, a million—all of them… I will touch them forever if you don't match me." Roxanne's voice fell to a whisper. "And soon, Billy. I don't usually go this long."

"How often?" I asked barely audible.

"Several times a night, Billy, until I stop hurting."

Roxanne's naked hand traveled to her throat as she

spoke and rested there. I was profanely interested in what *she* felt when she touched the college boys to death. Thankfully, that question did not leave my mouth.

"A match can absorb my touch, Billy. A match ends up saving lives."

"So you've had one before," I asked and she nodded. "What happened to the last one?"

"He died of old age. He was with me for forty-five years." Roxanne pulled off her left glove and dropped them both to the floor. "It can be a nice life, Billy. I have land, houses, boats, cars, anything you want. For as long as you live."

"There's gotta be a catch. I mean, I think you just caused Jasper's death." I blinked trying to make sense of it.

"No, Billy, no. Jasper knew my chance with the other man was blown. He also knew that I'd tested you already in my room and that you passed. Jasper is my former match's son. He hoped to take his father's place."

Roxanne's countenance darkened with sadness and I took a deep breath.

"Jasper was trying to commit suicide just now? That's why he was standing in the road?"

Roxanne shrugged and then nodded, her eyes never leaving mine.

"You just let him do it?" I asked in a whisper, almost speechless but not quite.

She shrugged and said nothing.

"Why would he do that? Why?" I asked, shaking my head. Yes, when she touched me, I nearly died with pleasure, but to stand in the road and wait for a car to run you over? Wasn't that insane?

"Because, Billy," Roxanne began as she grasped

the hem of her tight top, "the match doesn't die when I touch him."

In a flash, she pulled the stretchy garment over her head and dropped it alongside the gloves. Underneath, she wore a thin scoop-necked tank, her pale skin as blemish-free and perfect as I suspected it would be. Was it just her fingers that caused such excitement in my flesh? What if she touched me with her elbow? Her shoulder? Her knee? Her lips?

"The match doesn't die," she repeated and pulled the pins from her hair.

As I watched, her gorgeous blonde tresses fell to her waist as full and as wavy as in my filthiest dream.

"You're not even twenty, Billy. You have a long life ahead of you, a looooooong life, with me." She reached out her naked hand and I protectively clamped down my folded arms.

"What would I have to do?" I asked, trying out the scenario in my head. That was okay, wasn't it? Just a little dry-run to see how the whole thing sat with me?

"Take those pills—all of them, and don't regret it. I will be here to make you my match. In the nick of time, I'll bring you back, and then you'll be able to survive my touch for the remaining years of your life."

I must have looked dubious for she stepped forward, landing in the moonlight streaming over my shoulder.

"Do you, well, would we, you know…"

"You are not a girl and he's not worthy of you," Jasper had said.

I stammered again. "I mean, can I… will you…"

I was babbling, too embarrassed to ask if she'd satisfy me as much as I did her. But didn't I have a right to know what I was getting myself into? I sought the right words, but Roxanne filled in the blanks and smiled.

"I'm not really a girl, Billy. We can't have intercourse the way your people do."

"You're a transsexual?" I whispered, my eyes taking in her curves, my disbelief evident.

She offered me a new grin, small and to the side, her eyes shimmering with affection. "No, I'm not a man, either. I'm something else. Something you've never seen before." She held up her hand and I held my breath. "Remember my touch—that's what you want. Remember?"

"Did you come from outer space?" I asked in a small voice, the sci-fi nerd inside begging her to say yes. Because then, I could announce inside, *"I KNEW IT! MULDER HAD IT RIGHT ALL ALONG!"*

But Roxanne tilted her chin ever so slightly to the right and replied, "There is no outer space, honey. This is it."

I shook my head—sure, she might just offer me a supernatural delight, but I couldn't let her flat-out lie simply because she wanted me to do her will. "I see it. Why would you say that? I've seen it."

"You see what we want you to see. A light show. That's all it is. Now, hurry. I need you now. Time is running out…"

A light show? That movie came to mind, the one where the man is born and raised on the air and finds out as an adult that his life is the production brainchild of one man—a mortal man.

"Are you even human?" I asked and she shook her head. Dammit, she was so beautiful and she needed me. So what if she lied, I mean, I can see the moon and its craters with the naked eye. I have seen the stars, not to mention the most trusted space agency on the planet has shown all of us incontrovertible proof that we are a speck in a limitless universe. What did this creature gain from telling me it was all made up? As if I would open a door and be a tiny bug in the locker room of giants (yes, that movie came to mind, too).

Roxanne exhaled as if about to pull back.

"Wait. I'm sorry. Can I feel it again? Just a tiny bit? Just to be sure?" I asked, no better than a druggie trying to choose life over death and death over life.

Roxanne didn't delay to put forth her pointer and touch my inner elbow. Arrows of delight raced through me with power and I fell to my knees. The contact was severed and I remained where I was, kneeling, staring into her face.

I was going to do it.

What did I have in my miserable life that even half measured up to what I could have with this probably celestial but surely inhuman goddess in the form of a delicious woman?

Roxanne smiled again, as if she sensed my concession, and she gestured for the bathroom. Drunkenly, I scrabbled to my feet. It would be fine to spend my life with Roxanne. I mean, I'd be helping her so she wouldn't have to suffer. And I'd be helping the world, who'd get to keep their loved ones safe from her wanton touch. It was a win-win all around. I reached the bath and yanked open the drawer.

My stash was gone.

Unbelieving, I looked in the cupboard below as a crash sounded two rooms down. *Aunt Edna!*

The realization almost crippled me. When I spun around to explain to Roxanne, she was gone. I bolted for my aunt's room and I reached it in four big strides.

On the lavender comforter atop her bed, my sweet old aunt lay sprawled out, convulsing and foaming at the mouth. A sheet of paper fluttered to the ground near her head as Roxanne covered Edna's face with her hands.

"LET HER GO!" I shouted, and clawed at Roxanne's white fingers. Immediately, I was disabled and fell backward, rapping my head hard on the end table. Through fuzzy and wavering vision, I watched Edna's body rise to meet Roxanne's hands. Her long fingers traveled down my aunt's chest, her torso, her hips, her thighs, and finally to her toes. Roxanne was reviving her, but this kind of healing was the kind that enslaved the resurrected.

It was useless trying to rise so I yelled for help; nothing came out. All I could do was watch, and by the time the other guests reached the room, drawn by the commotion, Aunt Edna was sitting up in bed, grinning like a Cheshire cat.

Roxanne stood back, her huge smile in place, and waited for Edna to crawl out of bed. The other guests rushed in to inquire about her health and she sent them away, thanking them for their attentions. No one bothered about the masked boy prostrate on the rug beside the bed. Was I invisible? Of course, I was. I always had been, ever since the car accident that stole my face.

I clutched at the errant sheet of stationery that rested near my head. In my aunt's old-lady scrawl, she'd written, "I can't do it anymore. I'm sorry, Billy. The B&B is yours, Edna."

I'd been a selfish idiot; I never saw this coming.

But Roxanne had.

Had she known all along?

If she was drawn to suicides, did she really stop off here by accident and coincidence? Or did she and Jasper come to our specific B&B because there were *two* potentially suicidal people living here? I glanced at the wall clock. Jasper had chastised Roxanne for not being able to wait an hour. *That* was an hour ago. Could this woman predict suicides that accurately? The questions kept rolling in and there were no answers for any of them.

When only the three of us remained in the room, Edna rolled off the bed and folded herself into Roxanne's open arms, her mouth making sounds a nephew should never hear from his aunt. The Gloved One's bare hands traveled across my aunt's back, caressing, seductive, conforming to her old-lady shape as if Edna was the most beautiful creature in the world. My aunt's thick cotton night gown reached the ground and Roxanne tugged it up. I'd seen enough.

"Stop, god, Aunt Edna! Get away from her!" I wanted to yell, but I couldn't move. It didn't matter. Neither of them paid me any mind.

"You are my match," Roxanne said in my aunt's ear, just loud enough for me to hear.

She kissed her cheek, her jaw, and then found her mouth. My aunt was in utter ecstasy, groaning with pleasure and gyrating her body in Roxanne's arms.

Then the siren whispered, "Whatever you want, just ask. I'll take care of you. I need you, Edna. I need you sooooo badddddly..."

Wait! Stop! That's my aunt! I wanted to shout, but I was still frozen from touching Roxanne uninvited.

With a smooth movement, and her arm across Edna's shoulder, Roxanne turned for the door. For a fleeting moment, my aunt looked at me, but her eyes had changed. Her brown eyes were now the palest blue, and I saw in her gaze that she didn't know me at all.

I shuddered and tried once more to make a noise; the tiniest whimper issued forth—some victory.

"Come to my room, Edna. Stay with me tonight.

Stay in my bed," Roxanne said near her ear. "I will hold you close and touch you all night. Tomorrow, we'll plan our new life together. And you will be happy…"

"Please, oh, yes, *pleeeeeease…*" Edna purred, hanging on to the creature's arms, her voice nothing like that of my sweet aunt.

"Yes, oh, yes," the Gloveless One answered.

My poor aunt—what did it mean for her? She'd spend the rest of her days absorbing the creature's toxic touch? Carrying her luggage? Tending her daily business as a tactile-addicted slave?

That was supposed to be my job.

What was I saying?

I was miserable and incorrigible—a horrible combination.

Roxanne led my aunt to the door and looked back my way. "Go on to my room, Edna. I'll be right behind you."

My aunt nodded, still in the happy trance evoked by Roxanne's touch. When Edna was gone, she closed the door with two shapely fingers.

"Don't worry, Billy," she said and approached me on the floor, her eyes shining. "I'll be touching you now."

"What? Don't…" I gasped, finally un-sticking my tongue.

"I don't need you anymore, Billy. I have my new match." She sent me an air kiss as she knelt to my side.

"But—please, Roxanne, I don't want to die!" I yelped, still struggling to form words around my semi-paralyzed palate.

"Don't worry, it'll feel marvelous," the creature named Roxanne said. She rolled her eyes closed and reached her bare palm toward my chest.

"I'll be Jasper!" I said, or maybe I only thought it.

She was making contact. *Here it comes.* I strained to move away but was pinned to the floor by my lack of muscle control.

Deftly, Roxanne maneuvered her fingers under the fabric and lay her fingers directly on my sternum. In that moment, I'd never been happier to die.

"I'll be your Jasper…" I said, that time, for certain, inside only.

But Roxanne reacted. I think her eye rounded a little. I think her lips parted. I think it occurred to her that I could do the job. After all, I was empathetic, intelligent, resilient, and introverted…

I relaxed and lay on the floor and watched the ceiling fan.

Let's face it, is it really ever going to get better than this?

I didn't see how. Soon enough, my body was singing, and everything went black. Will she make me her Jasper? Will I wake up in time to carry her and Edna's suitcases?

If she doesn't bring me back, will I get back my face in heaven? It's a legitimate question, after all.

The E*N*D

More Delicious Works by your Tiny Tales Authors:

ELLEN C. MAZE

Check out Ellen's #1 Top-Rated Vampire Thriller
Winner of FIVE Readers' Favorite 5-Star Seals
RABBIT: CHASING BETH RIDER
https://www.amazon.com/dp/B0047GN9DI

The Corescu Chronicles, 5 Books in All
https://www.amazon.com/gp/product/B07KJS2Z4K
"It's DEXTER with fangs!" 5-stars! Amazon Reviewer

The Bone Spirit by Chris Snider

TAYLOR VOGT

Storm Orphans by Matt Handle

Proxima g by Victoria Williams

EMIL STERN (as EMIL JERSEY)

Malcontent by Emil Jersey

Darcy Vandiver Vampire Sexpert, A Memoir by Emil Jersey

Blood, Sex & Violence, a Vampire's Rebuttal by Emil Jersey

Meet your Tiny Tales Authors

(In alphabetical order)

1. Katie Barnett

Katie Barnett lives in Alabama with her family and pets. Writing has always been a large part of her life and after the birth of her daughter she decided to pursue a writing career. She can be found and contacted at fb.me/KatieBarnettAuthor.

2. Faye Brooks

K **FAYE BROOKS: Pen Name for Melinda S Reynolds** lives in South-West Kentucky. She is married with two sons, and three grandchildren

Mrs. Reynolds started out as an artist, then began writing fan fiction for the popular TV series **STAR TREK**; she edited, co-wrote, and printed the fanzine **DELTA TRIAD.** Aside from miscellaneous short stories, her current projects are the **ANGEL WARRIORS** and the **ANGEL ALEILAH** book series.

She has had artwork and fiction published in several ezines, fanzines, and books, as well as designing book covers for other artists. Her artwork has been on display and won awards at many local events. She designed, made, and displayed period clothing for the Henderson, KY, Bicentennial in 1992. Her hobby is designing and making costumes.

Currently retired, she spends her time drawing, writing, and serving as Treasurer for the Poole Volunteer Fire Department.

FACEBOOK: **Melinda S Reynolds**

3. Batya Dulos

A technical copyrighter by trade, as she approached retirement, Batya made a career change to editing speculative fiction. In 2019, she was hired as Chief Editor for Little Roni Publishers new Imprint, Run Rabbit Books.

4. Kay Fondren

Kay Fondren a.k.a., Delilah has been a published Author since 2012, though her writing began in the early 1970's. She was a syndicated advice columnist known as, "Dear Delilah' for two Newspapers, The Western Star and The Tannehill News. As an author she follows no specific genre or subject matter. Her imagination guides her hand when writing. She has authored books delving into horror, romance, biographical, humor, explicit adult reading, light mystery and Christian. You may find her on her Facebook Page: Delilah Kay Fondren and see her add-on page: Novel Ideas By Delilah & her WebSite: http://novelideasbydelilah.webs.com

5. Matt Handle

Visit author Matt Handle at his blog, "**riff:** ramblings, inklings, and flash fiction from author Matt Handle," at https://matthandle.blogspot.com/

6. Elizabeth E. Little

Author/Illustrator Elizabeth E. Little has been acknowledged internationally for her poetry and wrote her first novel at age thirteen. With literally tens of thousands of readers following her FanFiction, so far, we've talked her into submitting wonderful short tales to our LRP anthologies. Find her stories in LRP's FECKLESS & RunRabbitBooks, TINY TALES.

7. Ellen C. Maze

Bestselling novelist Ellen C. Maze finds writing fun and cathartic. Raised on Bram Stoker and Stephen King, Ellen takes the fantasy/ paranormal/ vampire genre directly into the heart of spiritual matters.

#1 Top-Rated by Amazon Customers & **2020 Gold Medal Best Book Award from ReadersFavorite.com:**
RABBIT: CHASING BETH RIDER (Book 1)

Also winning 5-star accolades, each book in the series:

RABBIT LEGACY (2)
RABBIT REDEMPTION (3)
ANOMALY (4)
CONUNDRUM (5)

Ellen's second 5-star Vampire Saga:
The Corescu Chronicles Book 1: THE JUDGING
The Corescu Chronicles Book 2: DAMASCUS ROAD
The Corescu Chronicles Book 3: TREE OF LIFE
The Corescu Chronicles Book 4: ANATHEMA
The Corescu Chronicles Book 5: NOVUS

VISIT THE AUTHOR AT www.ellencmaze.com, email her at ellenmaze@aol.com. Sign up for email alerts for promos and new releases at https://dl.bookfunnel.com/z0c7dpe1am

8. Chris Snider

"My name is Chris Snider. I'm a thirty-four-year-old writer who has Asperger's syndrome. I am a Christian and my first book was very Christian based, though I write mostly in the Horror genre. My favorite Authors are Dean Koontz, Nora Roberts, and Tami Hoag. My hobbies include, of course, reading and writing, but also video games and the NFL. I've always been fond of RPG games and survival horror games. My favorite NFL team is the Baltimore Ravens and I try to never miss a game. I am the author of 5 books on Amazon and one short story."

9. Emil Stern (with DH Lee)

A prolific fanfiction author, Emil Stern made his debut as "Emil Jersey," with the novel "Blood, Sex & Violence, a Vampire's Rebuttal," inspired by his enjoyment of The Rabbit Saga characters from a Run Rabbit Books series of the same name. Emil and his longtime writing partner, DH Lee, have many more stories to write and ask you to follow "Emil Jersey" on Amazon to be alerted of every new book. The author maintains a personal website at emiljersey.com and enjoys interacting with readers and friends on Facebook (Author Emil Jersey) and at Twitter handle, @EmilJerseyAF.

10. Taylor Vogt

Taylor Vogt is a 30-year-old Master of Fine Arts in creative writing student at Manhattanville College. He is also a sustainable energy expert, with a Master of Science in environmental policy and sustainability management from the New School. His writing passion is superhero stories. He is an active member of Twitter's #writingcommunity, works as an intern in resident for the Hudson Valley Writer's Center and has taught emerging writer's workshops. He is also an avid snowboarder and loves cats.
https://twitter.com/taylorevogt

11. Victoria Williams

Victoria is life-long student in a plethora of topics including mythology, history, science, music, and linguistics, and she utilizes these interests to enrich the stories she creates within her fantasy worlds. When not writing, Victoria can often be found lost somewhere among the many forests and mountains spread across North America, holding a book in her hands, or sitting with a cat nestled in her lap. You can see her work published in such places as Stone of Madness Press, Sienna Solstice Journal, and the Indie Voice Review. Find Victoria on Twitter @scinerd28 and Instagram @vwilliamsauthor

www.ingramcontent.com/pod-product-compliance
Lightning Source LLC
LaVergne TN
LVHW050641100826
845148LV00011B/1942

* 9 7 8 1 7 3 4 0 4 7 4 9 3 *